POOR MURDERER

Pavel Kohout, one of Czechoslovakia's leading dramatists and poets, was born in Prague on July 20, 1928. He earned his doctorate in philosophy at Karls University, Prague, and began his professional career as a journalist and radio reporter. For two years he was cultural attaché at his country's embassy in Moscow. While he was editor in chief of the satirical magazine *Dikobraz,* his lyric poetry made him the idol of Czechoslovakia's youth. As a consequence of his being one of the cultural leaders of the Prague spring of 1968, his works—including *The White Book in Matters of Adam Juracek* (from his novel *The Diary of a Counterrevolutionary*), *Evol, Poor Murderer, Roulette,* and *August, August, August* —have been suppressed by the Czech authorities. He has been denied a passport, and his works cannot be published or performed in his native country.

Poor Murderer

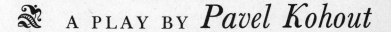 A PLAY BY *Pavel Kohout*

Translated by Herbert Berghof and Laurence Luckinbill

PENGUIN BOOKS

Penguin Books Ltd, Harmondsworth,
Middlesex, England
Penguin Books, 625 Madison Avenue,
New York, New York 10022, U.S.A.
Penguin Books Australia Ltd, Ringwood,
Victoria, Australia
Penguin Books Canada Limited, 2801 John Street,
Markham, Ontario, Canada L3R 1B4
Penguin Books (N.Z.) Ltd, 182–190 Wairau Road,
Auckland 10, New Zealand

First published in a German translation, *Armer Mörder*,
from the original Czech play, *Ubohý Vrah*, 1972
World publication rights controlled by
Reich Verlag AG, Lucerne, Switzerland
First published in the United States of America
in simultaneous hardcover and paperback editions by
The Viking Press (A Richard Seaver Book)
and Penguin Books 1977

LIBRARY OF CONGRESS CATALOGING IN PUBLICATION DATA
Kohout, Pavel.
Poor murderer.
Translation of *Armer Mörder* originally written in
Czech under title: *Ubohý Vrah*.
I. Title.
PG5038.K64U213   1977b   891.8'6'25   76-58851
ISBN 0 14 048.141 9

Printed in the United States of America by
Book Press, Brattleboro, Vermont
Set in Linotype Baskerville

First English-language performance on July 11, 1975,
at the H B Playwrights Foundation Theatre, New York, New York
First performance on Broadway on October 20, 1976,
presented by Kermit Bloomgarden, John Bloomgarden, and Ken Marsolais,
under the direction of Herbert Berghof

Amateur or professional performances, public readings,
and radio or television broadcasts of this play are forbidden
without permission in writing. All inquiries
concerning performing rights should be addressed to
Joan Daves, 515 Madison Avenue, New York, New York 10022.

Photographs by Frederic Ohringer

Contents

❧ Cast of Characters

PROFESSOR DRZHEMBITSKY

ANTON IGNATYEVICH KERZHENTSEV
    also Hamlet

ALEXEY KONSTANTINOVICH SAVELYOV—FIRST ACTOR
    also Polonius
        Hamlet II

TATYANA NIKOLAYEVNA—FIRST ACTRESS
    also Queen

SECOND ACTOR
    also Ignat Antonovich Kerzhentsev
        Rector
        Waiter
        Bernardo
        and others

THIRD ACTOR
  also Dean
       Lawyer
       Major Count Byelitsky
       Kurganov
       King
       and others

FOURTH ACTOR
  also Cashier
       Newspaper Vendor
       Conductor
       Gypsy
       Francisco
       Polonius II
       and others

SECOND ACTRESS
  also Servant Girl, Katya
       Flower Vendor
       Gypsy Roma
       Marya Vassilyevna
       and others

THIRD ACTRESS
  also Voluptuous Mistress
       Irina Pavlovna Kurganova
       Countess Byelitskaya
       and others

FOURTH ACTRESS
  also Slim Mistress
       Duchess de Cliche-Turomel
       Prologue
       and others

APPRENTICE
  also Gypsy Girl

FOUR ATTENDANTS

TWO or THREE MUSICIANS

PLACE and TIME: St. Petersburg, 1900

First English-language performance on July 11, 1975, at the H B Playwrights Foundation Theatre, New York.

First performance on Broadway on October 20, 1976, produced by Kermit Bloomgarden, John Bloomgarden, and Ken Marsolais under the direction of Herbert Berghof.

Act I

A room—wallpapered, all white—no windows.

In the center, a low platform—an improvised stage: portals and wings, quickly hammered together from boards and wooden beams; a front curtain and cyclorama made of strips of white linen sewn together. Now open, they reveal furniture stacked against the back wall. In the center of the platform, a prop basket.

On one side of the stage—the stage-within-a-stage— there is a long clothes rack; on it hang jackets, liveries, uniforms, and other costumes. On the other side, music stands and chairs. In the room there are also a number of chairs, obviously meant for an audience; around the platform are stands holding simple spotlights.

A door, at first not noticeable, opens, and a very elegantly dressed man, between thirty and forty years old, enters. With him are four strong-looking men in loose-fitting white trousers, shirts, and jackets; their behavior reveals a curious mixture of indifference and submissiveness. The elegant man has a sheaf of papers in his hand and refers to them as he checks off the costumes. Then he goes to the furniture on the platform as if to take inventory. The four Attendants watch him silently. He goes to the basket, bends over it, and checks the props. He straightens up and turns to one of the Attendants.

KERZHENTSEV: Where is the sword? The sword is missing.

ATTENDANT: We took what they gave us, Your Excellency.

KERZHENTSEV: But on the list it says "sword." (*He points to the paper.*) Here, look!

ATTENDANT: I can't read, Your Excellency.

KERZHENTSEV: Oh! You can't read? Well, I can! Here it says—"one sword." And right underneath—"sent out." And this is the stamp of the Royal Theatre. You understand? The official stamp! Now I've got you! Where is the sword?

ATTENDANT: In the prop room of the theatre, Your Excellency.

KERZHENTSEV: Don't lie!

ATTENDANT: Eh, we were ordered to return it, Your Excellency.

KERZHENTSEV: Who ordered it? I give the orders here!

ATTENDANT: The Professor, Your Excellency—

KERZHENTSEV: Oh, the Professor, I see. That means there are no knives, forks, or spoons here either, huh?

ATTENDANT: It was ordered that we return them, Your Excellency.

KERZHENTSEV (*Nods, goes on comparing the list with the contents of the basket*): Why are there no real cups, plates and glasses?

ATTENDANT: The Professor said here at the Institute . . .

KERZHENTSEV: What does the learned Professor have against plates and glasses? I ordered very cheap ones so they could be broken. It's one of the scenic high points! It's a matter of the right sound effect. No, no, just tell him under these circumstances . . .

(*The Attendant takes a bag out of the basket and smacks it with his hand. There is a sound of shattered glass and china. Kerzhentsev is suddenly resigned.*)

All right, all right . . . close the curtain and get ready for the first scene of my play. Scene One—my room as a child. And remember: if you miss one curtain cue, or one chair is out of place, I'm going to have you locked up in the security ward with the violent cases!

(*Two of the Attendants close the curtain in front of the platform. They disappear behind it, and we hear furniture being moved. Kerzhentsev turns to the other two Attendants.*)

Why don't you go and help them!
ATTENDANT: The Professor said we should not leave you.
KERZHENTSEV: All right. All right . . . I'll go with you.

(*All three disappear behind the curtain. The white door opens again and the Professor comes in: he is old, but tall and powerful, and in some manner resembles the Attendants. He is followed by a group of men and women dressed in clothes of 1900. Three of them carry musical-instrument cases. They look around, indecisive.*)

PROFESSOR (*To the Musicians*): Right here. This way please.

(*The Musicians take their places at music stands and begin unpacking their instruments and music scores.*)

(*To the First Actor and First Actress*): Over there, if you please. (*He points to two chairs on the side, half in darkness. They go to them and sit.*)

(*To the others*): And you, wherever you wish.

(*The others scatter to various chairs facing the stage and take out their rolled-up scripts. Everybody is noticeably tense.*)

(*The Professor claps his hands*): The actors of the Royal Theatre are here. You can begin!

(*From behind the curtain, the hand clap is repeated. Two Attendants appear again and draw the curtain. In the center of the platform Kerzhentsev; at either side of him the two Attendants.*)

KERZHENTSEV (*Friendly*): "You're welcome, gentlemen, welcome all!" (*Turning to the Second Actor*): "I'm glad to see you well."

(*Surprised, the Second Actor turns to the Professor.*)

PROFESSOR: You know him, Mr. Kerzhentsev?
KERZHENTSEV: "My old friend! Why thy face is valanced since I saw thee last; comest thou to beard me here?"

(*To Second Actress*): "What my young lady and mistress: you're nearer to heaven than when I saw you last, by the altitude of a chopine."

(*The Second Actress, too, is quite nonplussed, but before the Professor can interfere, Kerzhentsev turns to all and says*):

Masters, you're all welcome. "We'll e'en to't like French falconers, fly at any thing we see: Speak the speech, I pray you, as I pronounced it to you, trippingly on the tongue: but if you mouth it, and saw the air too much with your hand, thus" . . . then I'm sorry to say . . . "I had as lief the town crier spoke my lines."

(*The Professor and the others open their scripts in confusion, looking for the line.*)

"Be not too tame neither, but suit the action to the word, the word to the action; so that you o'erstep not the modesty of nature: for anything so overdone is from the purpose of playing, whose end, both at the first and now, was and is, to hold as 'twere, the mirror up to nature."

FIRST ACTOR: *Hamlet!*

PROFESSOR: You skipped over the beginning, Mr. Kerzhentsev!

KERZHENTSEV: "And let those that play your clowns speak no more than is set down for them."

PROFESSOR: This is your manuscript and in it Hamlet speaks only at the end.

KERZHENTSEV: Where is the end of a circle, Professor Drzhembitsky? And where is the beginning of my end? Anyway, why do my play at all?

PROFESSOR: It was your idea, Mr. Kerzhentsev. These

actors have kindly volunteered to perform your play and I have set up everything exactly the way you wanted it.

KERZHENTSEV: But why do it at all if you've already decided that I'm insane? We might as well play *Hamlet*.

PROFESSOR: I don't understand why you are so distrustful.

KERZHENTSEV: You don't understand? Where is my sword?

PROFESSOR: Here at St. Elizabeth Institute orders must be obeyed. Don't ask for anything impossible. Even within the framework of what *is* possible, your means are more than sufficient. I saw you die very often on the stage—let me remind you of your "Christian" in *Cyrano* —you convinced me every time. Why shouldn't you succeed as well now? Or don't you believe in yourself anymore?

KERZHENTSEV: Yes, I do. I do believe in myself.

PROFESSOR: Then let's begin! The actors are ready, you and I are ready. We all have imagination enough.

KERZHENTSEV (*Discovering the First Actor and the First Actress in the darkness*): Yes, yes . . . Oh, I'm sorry, I didn't notice you two were already here. I'm Kerzhentsev, Anton Ignatyevich Kerzhentsev—yes, the very same. I thank you for taking the trouble to come here. I don't think you'll regret it. My honored friends, I have kept the story of my life a secret until today. But now that I see how crucial it is to tell the truth, I will not withhold so much as my thoughts from you. I must speak. (*Turning to the Attendants at his side*): Leave me alone! (*They don't move.*) "I am but mad north-north-west: when the wind is southerly . . . I know a hawk from a handsaw."

FIRST ACTOR: Act Two, Scene Two.

KERZHENTSEV (*Picking up on it*): Oh, you know that? You love the theatre? Then ask the Professor to clear

our little stage—or we'll go on forever playing two plays
at once.

PROFESSOR (*Giving a signal to the Attendants to move
the portals*): There you are, Mr. Kerzhentsev.

KERZHENTSEV: Merci. Voilà, messieurs. Alors! (*He snaps
his fingers, and one of the Attendants strikes the gong.
Kerzhentsev rises.*) Dearest friends! You are now going
to witness the life of a man who believed in only one
thing: Reason. The entire history of mankind seemed
to him one victorious march of Reason from the very
moment his innocence was so terribly betrayed—who's
playing the part of my father?

SECOND ACTOR: I, maestro.

KERZHENTSEV: You know me?

SECOND ACTOR: How should I not know you, maestro?

KERZHENTSEV: We traveled together?

SECOND ACTOR: We played together.

KERZHENTSEV: Cards? Roulette?

SECOND ACTOR: We rehearsed *Hamlet* together.

PROFESSOR: You don't remember, Mr. Kerzhentsev?

KERZHENTSEV: No, Professor. (*He laughs.*) I've never
seen this man before.

SECOND ACTOR: I played Bernardo, Reynaldo, and For-
tinbras, maestro. I had a different beard in every scene.

PROFESSOR: Do you believe it now, Mr. Kerzhentsev?

KERZHENTSEV: Excuse me. Let me see, my father . . .
(*Goes to costume rack, picks out a very modish jacket
and a top hat.*) Put this on. This is the way you are
engraved in my memory since that special day when
Katya first took me with her to your courtroom.
Where's Katya?

SECOND ACTRESS: Katya, the servant girl?

KERZHENTSEV: There was only one.

SECOND ACTRESS: What do I wear?

KERZHENTSEV: The same as Katya wore the first time I

saw her, and the last. Nothing, nothing at all. (*Starts to laugh.*)

SECOND ACTRESS (*To Professor*): Forgive me, but . . . I'm not going to take my . . .

KERZHENTSEV: Never mind, stay the way you are. (*Laughs.*) We all have more imagination than we need.

SECOND ACTRESS: But . . .

KERZHENTSEV (*Claps his hands*): S'il vous plaît! La musique numéro un!

(*One of the Musicians plays the Orthodox Credo. Kerzhentsev takes off his jacket and pulls his shirt out of his trousers. The Second Actor steps onto the platform.*)

SECOND ACTOR: Anton . . . (*He stops, taken aback.*)

KERZHENTSEV: Did you forget your lines?

SECOND ACTOR: Excuse me, there should be a child here . . .

KERZHENTSEV: That's me. I'm ten years old, and you just burst into my room. Go ahead!

SECOND ACTOR: Anton, on your knees! Repent! (*Takes off his belt.*)

KERZHENTSEV (*Falls on his knees and folds his hands in supplication*): Papa, no! Papa, what did I do?

SECOND ACTOR: That's what I'm asking *you*. Confess, and I'll have mercy on you if you vow, on your life, that this will never—do you hear me, never—happen again.

KERZHENTSEV: I don't know what I did.

SECOND ACTOR: You don't? Well, I do! Did you or didn't you stand there in the corner in front of the mirror?

KERZHENTSEV: No, I swear I didn't!

SECOND ACTOR: No? You swear? That's perjury. You stood in front of the mirror and you committed a lewd sexual act on yourself.

KERZHENTSEV: No. No!

SECOND ACTOR: You won't admit it. Do you think you can lie to me because you were alone in the room? You were not alone, Anton, your mother saw you!

KERZHENTSEV (*Terrified*): My mother!

SECOND ACTOR: Yes, your dear departed mother rose from her grave and cried out to me that you are soiling her memory, and because of your sins, she has to suffer in hell. Do you hear me? In hell!

KERZHENTSEV: No . . .

SECOND ACTOR: Yes. Her hands have been pierced with rusty nails, and her feet scalded in boiling oil. And now I will punish you for your disgrace and her pain! (*He hits the chair next to Kerzhentsev with his belt.*)

KERZHENTSEV: No, no! Please don't! I won't ever do it again! Never! I'd rather—much rather—suffer in hell myself.

SECOND ACTOR (*Throws away the belt*): Shame! Anton! Shame! Now you go and pray to God and to your dear mother, until they both give you a sign that they for-

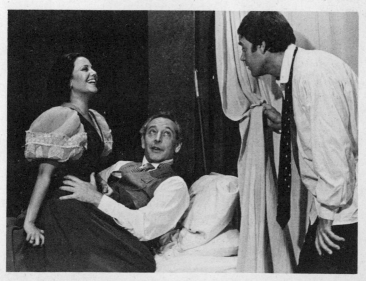

give you. And remember—they tell me everything. Do you hear? Everything! (*Goes behind curtain.*)

KERZHENTSEV (*Crosses himself and hits his head against the floor*): Great God, merciful God, have mercy on miserable me who lives in deadly sin and has forgotten you! Mother, my dear mother, I swear by all the holy saints, I'm going to do everything so that you can return to the holy angels in heaven! I will honor your memory as father does. I will be good, I won't be naughty, I will be obedient. I will be humble . . . I will . . .

(*For quite a while the laughter of a man and a woman is heard from behind the curtain. Kerzhentsev raises his head and the Credo stops. The creaking noises of a bed are heard underneath the two voices.*)

SECOND ACTOR: So . . . so . . . so . . . so . . .

SECOND ACTRESS: You you you you you . . . Aaaaaaah!!!!

SECOND ACTOR: Aaaaaaah! Who taught you that, you witch?

SECOND ACTRESS: You did! I saw your son in front of the mirror. This family knows everything!

SECOND ACTOR (*Laughs*): You want to stay here with me, you blessed little saint.

SECOND ACTRESS (*Laughs*): Yes, I come straight from hell and—suffered!

(*Kerzhentsev tears open the curtain. Behind it, on a bed, the Second Actor and the Second Actress are lying in an embrace.*)

SECOND ACTOR: Anton . . . what are you doing here? . . . Why are you looking at me that way? This is Katya, our new maid. I'm just looking her over to see whether she's healthy.

SECOND ACTRESS: Does the young gentleman wish anything?

KERZHENTSEV (*Draws the curtain*): "To die, to sleep;
To sleep: perchance to dream: aye, there's the rub;
For in that sleep of death what dreams may come,
When we have shuffled off this mortal coil."
. . . that's what we don't know . . . "That makes calamity of so long life" . . .

FIRST ACTOR (*Sotto voce to First Actress*): Act Three, Scene One!

PROFESSOR: Mr. Kerzhentsev, how can a child quote Hamlet?

KERZHENTSEV (*Stuffing his shirt back in his trousers*) : Hamlet is a child in the beginning just as I was, Professor. Where does the child end, and where does Hamlet begin? Where does Hamlet end, and where does the madman begin? And where does the madman end, and where do I begin? That is the question. C'est la question. (*He returns to the curtain and pushes it aside. The two Actors still wait there undecided what to do. To Second Actor*) : Did you ever play Mark Antony?

SECOND ACTOR: I never had the honor, maestro.

KERZHENTSEV: But you do know the funeral oration over Caesar's corpse?

SECOND ACTOR: How could I not know it, maestro? (*He takes a deep breath as if to begin.*)

KERZHENTSEV: You don't have to say the words! Just hold the pose in which you would have done the speech. (*Second Actor assumes an extreme theatrical pose. Kerzhentsev laughs.*) Yes, that's exactly how my father looked the first time I saw him in court. Your speeches brought the Prosecutors to despair . . . and moved all the ladies present to tears. But I knew you existed only from the tonsils out, only in tones and gestures. Very often I asked myself whether you existed at all. (*To the Professor*): He couldn't even understand that he was living and some day would be dead. When he went to bed at night, he simply stopped moving. In the morning, he got up without dreams, without doubts, like an animal . . . (*To Second Actor*): And yet everybody believed you had an extraordinary intellect, and you yourself never hesitated to tell me that if you weren't such a famous lawyer, then you . . . well, then you'd be . . . Scene Three, friend. You are invading my bedroom again.

(*Kerzhentsev lies on the bed.*)

SECOND ACTOR: Come in! Mesdames, come now, and don't be frightened! This isn't a prison cell, it's my son's bedroom. Anton! (*Waking him up roughly*) Get up!

KERZHENTSEV (*Shielding his eyes*): Bonjour, Papa.

SECOND ACTOR: You hear that? Papa! Oui, c'est mon fils. That's my son. Would you believe it? Look at him, ladies! Every hair in place, even when he sleeps. It spoils my appetite . . . for food, or anything else.

THIRD ACTRESS: Then let's muss him up a little bit!

KERZHENTSEV: The teachers want us to be properly groomed.

SECOND ACTOR: Do you hear that? The teachers! At his age . . . I had already taken all my female teachers into the woods.

FOURTH ACTRESS: Mais, c'est un beau garçon! Give him some vodka!

KERZHENTSEV: I don't drink.

SECOND ACTOR: Did you hear that? He doesn't drink, he doesn't smoke, he doesn't dance, he just stares and whines. With whom did your mother sleep to produce you? Me? It couldn't have been me, God knows. I'm a famous lawyer! And if I weren't, I could be an even more famous—actor. Just like that!

FOURTH ACTRESS: Ignát, why don't you leave me alone with him and I'll teach him. (*She kisses Kerzhentsev.*)

KERZHENTSEV: What are you doing?

FOURTH ACTRESS: That's a kiss, mon petit. Did it hurt?

KERZHENTSEV: I have to do my homework in the morning.

SECOND ACTOR: Do you hear that? Homework! (*He picks up some school notebooks.*) There is not one mistake in his homework, not one inkspot, not one crooked line. How could he be mine? (*He throws the notebooks up in the air.*) My God, what did I do to deserve such a son?

THIRD ACTRESS: Don't upset yourself, Ignátjuschka!

FOURTH ACTRESS: Mon amour! Ne t'agite pas!

(*The women embrace the Second Actor. He puts his arms around them and they exit—he is cursing, they are laughing.*)

KERZHENTSEV (*Collecting his notebooks*): If he had looked carefully, he would have found only one sentence, without mistakes or inkspots, repeated a thousand times.

PROFESSOR (*Taking the notebook that Kerzhentsev hands him. Reads*): "My father is a mean, lying rat."

KERZHENTSEV (*Laughs*): Yes! He had no idea, my friends, that it was I who could have been an infamous lawyer or a famous actor: he believed me when I pretended to have no talents.

SECOND ACTRESS (*Crossing the stage. Teasingly*): Does the young gentleman wish anything?

KERZHENTSEV: Yes . . . yes! But I had to suppress that wish for many years. Until the night his bed stopped squeaking from the rigors of love, and he lay forever unmoving—a corpse.

(*Second Actor lies down on the bed, hands folded, corpselike. Second Actress is crying at his feet. The Attendants place two candles near the bed. The harmonium plays.*)

My learned friends, what drives me to his room now might seem to you just childish and stubborn. To me it is a matter of life or death. I'm so terrified I could vomit, because I know if I falter—if I discover that I'm a coward—I'll kill myself.

(*Second Actress begins praying. Kerzhentsev circles the dead man's bed and kneels facing her.*)

SECOND ACTRESS: Does the young gentleman . . . The young gentleman will forgive me . . . I just wanted to say goodbye.

KERZHENTSEV: Yes.

SECOND ACTRESS: We both loved him.

KERZHENTSEV: Yes. (*He slowly unbuttons his shirt.*)

SECOND ACTRESS: Why does the young gentleman look at me so?

KERZHENTSEV: Don't you know, Katya?

SECOND ACTRESS: No. (*She straightens her dress, wipes her eyes.*) Does the young gentleman care for anything?

KERZHENTSEV: How long have you been with us?

SECOND ACTRESS: This is the ninth year, young gentleman.

KERZHENTSEV: You were nineteen then, and I was ten. And you've loved him all this time?

SECOND ACTRESS (*Wants to get up*): Young gentleman . . .

KERZHENTSEV (*Reaches across the corpse for her hand*): Speak, Katya! This is the night for truth.

SECOND ACTRESS: Yes . . . (*She begins to cry.*)

KERZHENTSEV: And he? Did he love you, too?

SECOND ACTRESS: I don't know.

KERZHENTSEV: And I? What have I meant to you these last nine years?

SECOND ACTRESS: You, you were the young gentleman . . . I did what I was ordered to do.

KERZHENTSEV: And if *I* had *ordered* you to do with me what you did with him?

SECOND ACTRESS: Young gentleman . . .

KERZHENTSEV: Should I answer for you? You would have gone to him, and complained about me.

SECOND ACTRESS: *You* would never have ordered me to do that!

KERZHENTSEV: Why do you think that?

SECOND ACTRESS: Because you're different.

KERZHENTSEV: How . . . different?

SECOND ACTRESS: Better.

KERZHENTSEV: Why didn't you love *me* then?

SECOND ACTRESS: If the young gentleman will permit me, I am going to sleep now.

KERZHENTSEV: I permit it . . . I permit it! You can sleep right now—right here—with me! (*He tears off his shirt.*)

SECOND ACTRESS: What are you doing? (*Crosses herself.*) You're committing a sin!

KERZHENTSEV: I love you. (*He crawls to her and embraces her legs passionately.*) Don't you know that? I've loved you since you came here . . . and I hate him because he had you and didn't love you. That's why I prayed for him to die!

SECOND ACTRESS (*Covering her ears*): I shouldn't listen to this! I mustn't!

KERZHENTSEV: You must . . . for nine years you never noticed me. You let him make love to you and you were nothing to him—just a servant girl. But I loved you, and

I prayed to God to punish him, and I swore to God that I would make up for your suffering a hundred times! And now the moment is here, and you don't want to hear it?

SECOND ACTRESS: I . . . I can't believe it.

KERZHENTSEV: Why not, Katya? Why not?

SECOND ACTRESS: But this isn't like you . . .

KERZHENTSEV: You think I can't love because I'm only nineteen? Katya, look into my eyes! I've never made love to anyone before, and "I swear" I will "never" love anyone but you. Would it be so bad if I held you in my arms?

SECOND ACTRESS: No . . . no . . .

KERZHENTSEV: Here I am!

SECOND ACTRESS: Yes . . . yes . . . (*She presses him to her bosom.*)

KERZHENTSEV: Give yourself to me . . . Give yourself to me.

SECOND ACTRESS: Not here . . . somewhere else . . .

KERZHENTSEV: Here. It's my right! This is the only way we can forget him—the only way I can forget that you were his for nine years. Come, let me take you.

SECOND ACTRESS: Yes.

(*She sinks down onto the bed. He falls on top of her, completely covering her. Then he raises his head, looks at the others, and starts to laugh.*)

KERZHENTSEV: And I took her . . . right in front of my father, to whom she wanted to be faithful beyond the grave. It was revenge for all his betrayals, for having loved him as much as I hated him. (*Stops laughing.*) And it was a threefold victory, my honored friends; over her, over him, and over myself. From that moment, I was certain I had that very talent for pretense which he would have been the last to grant me. And what a talent! (*He gets up, steps in front of the dead man, and crosses his arms triumphantly.*)

SECOND ACTRESS (*Sighs, and opens her arms to him*): Antonuschka! Beloved!

KERZHENTSEV: Get out of my house, you whore!

(*Second Actress screams and faints. A gong sounds. The Attendants remove the candles and the bed. The Second Actor leaves the platform and sheds his jacket. The Second Actress gets up and pages through her script.*)

Just let me add, Professor, that I immediately took a bath and then looked into the mirror for a long time—at my eyes. For the first time, I noticed how black they were, how beautiful, how confidence-inspiring. No wonder Katya had believed me. And yet more than anything, I was proud that I had absolutely no remorse. I stayed reasonable and detached: *that* was exactly what I had wanted to prove to myself. (*Turns to Second Actress*): Je vous remercie, mademoiselle. C'est tout.

PROFESSOR: Katya is a very interesting role. Can't we see more of her? Why does she end so abruptly?

KERZHENTSEV: Well, after both funerals, I went to Petersburg.

PROFESSOR: After both . . . ?

KERZHENTSEV: To study medicine.

PROFESSOR: Do you mean to say that Katya . . . ?

KERZHENTSEV: I mean to say that my father in his Last Will and Testament took an unexpected revenge on me: He withheld my inheritance until the day of my graduation. I was condemned for five more years to the role of a struggling, poverty-stricken student, and only the power of my special talent saved me: I identified myself so completely with that role that I escaped despair, but my brain, poised like a harpoon, lay in wait for its chance to get my revanche.

(*He has by now put on a student uniform, and steps onto the platform, which has been changed to student quarters, and bends to his homework. The Third Actor puts on a pince-nez. The Fourth Actor puts on cashier's sleeve-covers and take up a ledger. The First Actor gets up and at the Professor's signal steps onto the platform, remaining hidden from Kerzhentsev behind the other two Actors. Gong.*)

THIRD ACTOR (*As the Dean*): Kerzhentsev!

KERZHENTSEV (*Quickly rises*): Dean . . .

THIRD ACTOR: I'm sorry to disturb you, especially in such an embarrassing matter. (*To the First and Fourth Actors*): This is the student Kerzhentsev in his sixth semester, one of our best, most honest students. Kerzhentsev, I'm sure you know this gentleman?

(*The Third and Fourth Actors now step aside. Kerzhentsev for the first time sees the First Actor face to face. He is stunned.*)

KERZHENTSEV: Good God, it's . . . ?

PROFESSOR (*Coming quickly to platform*): Do you recognize him?

KERZHENTSEV: But that is—

THIRD ACTOR (*Continuing as per his script*): Yes, that is Alexey Konstan—

PROFESSOR: Now, just a moment please! (*To Kerzhentsev*): Do you remember?

KERZHENTSEV: Alexey Konstantinovich Savelyov!

PROFESSOR (*As excited as the others*): But then . . .

KERZHENTSEV (*Suddenly turning to the Third Actor*): Isn't that the gentleman who just played *The Pranks of Scapin* for us in the school auditorium?

THIRD ACTOR (*Continuing from his script*): Yes, the

same. Mr. Savelyov is, of course, not only a famous actor, but also . . .

PROFESSOR: Not another word, monsieur.

THIRD ACTOR (*Confused*): But it's in my script . . .

PROFESSOR: Mr. Kerzhentsev, if you would like to stop at this point . . .

KERZHENTSEV: Yes, yes . . . (*Turning to the First Actor*): Mr. Prosecuting Attorney, I want to thank you for participating personally in this truth game by assuming the role of Alexey Savelyov. Of course, I understand you want to get to know me at close quarters. With your help, I will certainly prove to the Professor how absurdly mistaken he is. And that was what you wanted, wasn't it Professor?

PROFESSOR (*Resigned*): I can only wish you success, Mr. Kerzhentsev. Please, let's continue!

KERZHENTSEV (*Turns to Third Actor*): Continue!

THIRD ACTOR (*Looks at Professor. At a nod from the Professor, he repeats the lines from his script*): Mr. Savelyov is not only a famous actor, but also the director of his theatre. He has taken the trouble to come here to clear up quite a different sort of "prank"—if one is inclined to call it that.

KERZHENTSEV: Enchanté, monsieur. Je suis à vous.

THIRD ACTOR: I've just told Mr. Savelyov that you received seventy-five rubles in admission fees from the student body for today's performance of *Scapin*. However, Mr. Savelyov's theatre cashier claims you gave him only sixty.

FOURTH ACTOR: Sixty, Director Savelyov! Not a kopeck more.

THIRD ACTOR: What have you to say to this, Kerzhentsev? Didn't you tell me yourself we took in seventy-five?

KERZHENTSEV: Yes, Dean. Seventy-five.

THIRD ACTOR: Well, this is amazing indeed, Kerzhentsev. To this day I have never caught you in so much as a lie, or even worse—yes, I would have to call it that—in an embezzlement.

KERZHENTSEV: I hope I won't disappoint you in the future, either, Dean.

THIRD ACTOR: Then . . . would you care to explain—?

KERZHENTSEV: No, I wouldn't like to explain. However, it's true that the amount received was seventy-five rubles.

THIRD ACTOR: And that's all you have to say?

FIRST ACTOR (*Who until now has been observing the room and Kerzhentsev*): Forgive me, Dean, if I'm interfering, but perhaps Kerzhentsev is trying very tactfully to say that he delivered to my cashier the exact amount he received.

FOURTH ACTOR: But, Director Savelyov—

KERZHENTSEV: Thank you for understanding me so completely, Mr. Savelyov.

THIRD ACTOR: How should I take this?

FIRST ACTOR (*Turning to Fourth Actor*): You're the cashier, don't you want to clarify this?

FOURTH ACTOR (*Goes to his knees, and wrings his hands*): Director Savelyov, it was the last time, I swear on my children's life, really the last time!

FIRST ACTOR: How often have I said, "I'll let it go this time, but just one more time and it's the last!"

FOURTH ACTOR: Have pity.

FIRST ACTOR: You're discharged! And you will have to make up the losses.

KERZHENTSEV: This grotesque incident showed me what a really inadequate actor I still was, because I nearly gave the whole thing away. I nearly took the fifteen rubles out of my pocket just to prove to myself I wasn't dreaming.

PROFESSOR: You mean you did have the money?

KERZHENTSEV: Of course! But how could I ever imagine that the cashier would confess to something he hadn't really done, just to get his usual pardon again.

FOURTH ACTOR: Director Savelyov, Director, I'll be ruined.

FIRST ACTOR: You've ruined yourself once and for all, by nearly ruining someone who was innocent.

FOURTH ACTOR (*Screams*): He is a common thief! I have a wife and children! He gave me only sixty rubles, I swear it!

FIRST ACTOR: If you say another word, I'll call the police! I think I have reason enough.

FOURTH ACTOR: Oh no, for God's sake, don't . . . ! For God's sake don't! (*He takes off his sleeve-covers and leaves, defeated.*)

FIRST ACTOR: I beg you, dear Mr. Kerzhentsev, to accept my deepest apology. If there is any way I can make up for this, I'll be happy to.

KERZHENTSEV: I have only one request, Mr. Savelyov. This is the very first time I've hurt someone unwillingly, and it will be difficult for me to forget the look in his eyes. Would you permit me to make up his debt out of my allowance? (*He takes money out of his pocket.*) Oh look, isn't that a sign from heaven! I happen to have fifteen rubles with me. What a coincidence.

FIRST ACTOR: There are so few good men in this world we shouldn't refuse them anything, especially a request like yours. The Dean will permit me, I'm sure, to invite you to the Theatre Club for lunch—that should help to make up for it.

THIRD ACTOR: Quite frankly, if it were another student, I wouldn't permit it. . . . I don't have to tell you, Kerzhentsev, that this is an expression of my deepest trust in you.

(*The Attendant who has been following the script hits the gong. Kerzhentsev puts his arm around the First Actor in a confidential manner and takes him off the platform while the scene is changed.*)

KERZHENTSEV: Of *his* trust, I was certain. Now, I only had to find out how I had fooled the other one.

FIRST ACTOR: Who?

KERZHENTSEV: Savelyov, of course, Mr. Prosecuting Attorney. He was an experienced actor, who only an hour before, on the stage, had fooled all of Molière's characters, and—I admit—even me in the audience, although I was extremely critical of all actors. But I had to test once more what I discovered the night my father died.

(*The Attendants have set up chairs and a table with a pitcher and tin cups. Another Attendant pours vodka. Kerzhentsev and the First Actor return to the platform and sit at the table.*)

Mr. Savelyov, why did you believe a completely unknown student? I could have lied to you more easily than your cashier.

FIRST ACTOR: Oh no, Mr. Kerzhentsev.

KERZHENTSEV: How could you be so sure?

FIRST ACTOR: I knew it the moment I stepped into your room.

KERZHENTSEV: Oh, if you judged me on the basis of the Spartan order in my room, may I point out to you that the best-kept rooms are occupied by prisoners.

FIRST ACTOR: Oh no, I judged it by something else.

KERZHENTSEV: What?

FIRST ACTOR (*Raising his cup*): Your eyes.

KERZHENTSEV (*He takes his cup, jumps up, and ex-*

citedly turns toward the Professor): You see, I was right! (*He sits again, sets the cup down, and pushes it away. To the First Actor*): I'm afraid you've invited rather poor company for lunch. If you read my eyes so well, then you must know that, among other things, I am a fanatic teetotaler.

FIRST ACTOR (*Drinks and snaps his fingers for a refill*): Maybe we've met just so I could help you overcome that problem.

KERZHENTSEV: I don't consider it a problem.

FIRST ACTOR: I admit, in the medical profession it's probably even an advantage. I certainly have much more confidence in a sober doctor. But do you really want to become a doctor?

KERZHENTSEV: Why shouldn't I?

FIRST ACTOR: I'm not saying that you shouldn't, but what if there is another talent within you, a talent that you don't even suspect you have . . .

KERZHENTSEV: What talent?

FIRST ACTOR: Just suppose the scalpel is less your métier than the prop sword.

KERZHENTSEV: You read all this in my eyes?

FIRST ACTOR: Scapin read it there. (*He toasts, signals for a refill.*)

KERZHENTSEV: Scapin?

FIRST ACTOR: Didn't you sit in the middle of the first row during the performance?

KERZHENTSEV: How did you know that? There were three hundred of us in the auditorium!

FIRST ACTOR: Didn't you have the feeling I was looking directly at you?

KERZHENTSEV: I suppose everybody in the audience has that feeling.

FIRST ACTOR: But an actor, Mr. Kerzhentsev, searches

among all the faces for the One—the one that will become his mirror—and when he finds it, he acts better than ever.

KERZHENTSEV: Why is that?

FIRST ACTOR: Because that face belongs to a man who feels the same way the actor does. You know Hamlet's advice to the players? The expression on that face immediately reveals to the actor when he is underplaying, or when he kills a fragile thought with too much pathos. I found such a face today in the middle of the first row. And that's why I would have believed *you*—even if my cashier had never stolen before. (*He toasts Kerzhentsev again.*)

KERZHENTSEV: A mirror? I don't understand how it's possible. I don't know anything about the theatre.

FIRST ACTOR: You never wanted to be an actor?

KERZHENTSEV: Never in my wildest dreams.

FIRST ACTOR: Maybe you are one and you don't know it. The longer I look at you, the more I believe it.

KERZHENTSEV: My late father believed I had no talent of any kind.

FIRST ACTOR: The tree was chopped down before the apple ripened.

KERZHENTSEV: I have to admit the theatre does have a very curious attraction for me. Still, I've never wanted to be anything but an honest doctor.

FIRST ACTOR: Would it surprise you to hear that I'm both a Doctor of Civil Law and a Doctor of Roman Law?

KERZHENTSEV: You? Then how did you become an actor?

FIRST ACTOR: Someone told me what I'm telling you. You see, the theatre attracts and needs those with a sixth sense. A talent for make believe. We can take a lie and turn it into the truth—truth into a lie. You have that talent. Don't let it lie fallow. In time, you may discover that I'm right. And I'll be happy to help you. (*Again raises his cup.*) To your talent, Mr. Kerzhentsev! (*Now they both drink.*) Oh, you did drink!

KERZHENTSEV (*With childlike astonishment*): Did I drink? (*They both laugh. Kerzhentsev get up and takes the First Actor off the platform.*) But I got *him* drunk, Mr. Prosecutor, and with the idea that he had discovered a spark in the ashes. For two years he wooed me with the secret rites of the art of acting, while I pretended to resist like a clever woman who knows the easiest way to catch a husband. (*He calls to the Musicians*): Numéro trois!

(*The Musicians now play a very festive melody. The Second Actor enters in the scholastic robe and chain of a Rector, flanked by two Attendants, who carry the insignias for the graduation.*)

SECOND ACTOR: Mr. Anton Ignatyevich Kerzhentsev, adhering to all requirements, is hereby made a Doctor of Medicine.

KERZHENTSEV: At last!

(*The Musicians play a flourish, and the Third Actor enters in a frock coat, with an open law book, flanked by two Attendants, who hold a Cross and a Statue of Justice.*)

THIRD ACTOR: Mr. Anton Ignatyevich Kerzhentsev, fulfilling all conditions, is hereby declared the sole heir of Ignat Antonovich Kerzhentsev.

KERZHENTSEV: At last! .

(*Fourth Actor enters as a newspaper vendor, papers under his arm.*)

FOURTH ACTOR (*Calls out*): Scandal in Petersburg Society! Kerzhentsev goes into the Theatre! Doctor Kerzhentsev, heir of Advocate Kerzhentsev, goes into the Theatre! Scandal in Petersburg Society!

KERZHENTSEV: At last!!

(*Behind the platform we see spotlights aimed toward us. Behind them, the faces of the Attendants and Actors as they applaud and shout "Bravo!" Kerzhentsev bows upstage toward them as the curtain closes. The First Actor runs to him and embraces him.*)

FIRST ACTOR: Anton! You've turned a scandal into a sensation. It is a success. A success!

KERZHENTSEV: Your success, Alexey Konstantinovich.

FIRST ACTOR: You were on stage, not I!

KERZHENTSEV: But it was your technique and your part.

FIRST ACTOR: Never mind! From the first moment I looked into your eyes, I knew: I have a comrade in arms.

KERZHENTSEV: Let's hope my eyes will never disappoint you.

(*He embraces him. The chandelier blazes with light. The Attendants bring in a deep armchair, and the Musicians play a waltz. The Third Actress hurries in, padded and corseted.*)

THIRD ACTRESS: Très bien! Magnifique! We were in raptures . . .

PROFESSOR: Pardonnez-moi, s'il vous plaît!

(*Music stops. Third Actress stops, undecided.*)

KERZHENTSEV (*Annoyed, turns*) : What is it?

PROFESSOR: I want to know one thing, Mr. Kerzhentsev: When you said to Mr. Savelyov, "Let's hope my eyes will never disappoint you," *was* that play-acting or truth?

KERZHENTSEV: "Play-acting"? In all my life, I had no other friend but him.

PROFESSOR: Then you really felt committed to him?

KERZHENTSEV: Committed? I needed him no more than he needed me.

PROFESSOR: For what did he need you?

KERZHENTSEV: When someone's star is fading, it's better

to discover the new one and before everyone else. Reflected glory, you know!

PROFESSOR: What made you think his star was fading?

KERZHENTSEV: He noticed mine, Professor, he noticed *mine*.

(*Kerzhentsev snaps his fingers, and the Musicians play the waltz again. The First Actor, a cup in his hand, sits in the armchair. The Third Actress runs to Kerzhentsev and shakes his hand. She continues as before.*)

THIRD ACTRESS: Très bien. Magnifique! We were in raptures, all of us. For the first time in my life, I really longed to be Juliet.

FIRST ACTOR: Not before now, madame? That's a pity.

THIRD ACTRESS (*Looks at him, flustered*): Oh, Alexey Konstantinovich . . . but then I thought of your Romeo, and I really didn't know whom I should like better.

FIRST ACTOR: Maybe one of the Capulets? (*He takes a cup from a passing Attendant and gulps it down.*)

THIRD ACTRESS: You are a bad boy. (*Offering her hand to Kerzhentsev to be kissed*): Irina Pavlovna Kurganova. Our house is open to you as well. We receive every Wednesday. Nous serons heureux de vous saluer . . .

(*She is swept aside by the elegant, wonderfully groomed Fourth Actress, who enters majestically.*)

FOURTH ACTRESS (*To Kerzhentsev*): Romeo! Romeo! Mes compliments, monsieur. Finally there is someone on our dreary stage who I believe would give life for love.

FIRST ACTOR: And unlike you, Duchess, his own.

FOURTH ACTRESS (*Coolly*): Now you see how dangerous it is to give away your own star parts so casually, mon cher.

FIRST ACTOR: You're wrong there, ma chère. Parts and

women leave on their own. (*He takes a cup from an Attendant and gulps it down.*)

FOURTH ACTRESS: As I see, you are in familiar company. Could you at least introduce me to your protégé?

FIRST ACTOR (*Rising with difficulty*): Excusez-moi . . . Anton Ignatyevich Kerzhentsev, my friend—the Duchess de Cliche-Turomel, my—the mistress of this house, and of all the guests.

FOURTH ACTRESS (*To Kerzhentsev*): Voulez-vous danser, monsieur?

KERZHENTSEV: I'm afraid three-quarter time is too fast for me.

FOURTH ACTRESS: I will lead you.

(*They dance away from Savelyov.*)

FIRST ACTOR: Bon voyage, mon ami! Pay my respects to all the old familiar places!

(*He takes another vodka and drinks it down with a melancholy air. Kerzhentsev dances with the Fourth Actress, who presses herself more and more closely to him.*)

KERZHENTSEV: I had the impression that he came here tonight because of you.

FOURTH ACTRESS: Oh, do you think so? But this is *your* evening, and since chance has brought you under my roof, it's up to me to see you're well taken care of.

KERZHENTSEV: It wasn't chance, Duchess, it was Alexey Konstantinovich.

FOURTH ACTRESS: Why don't you leave it to me, monsieur, what steps to take? After all, an invitation to dance is not yet an invitation to confess all your secrets to me . . . anyhow, what are we talking about? (*The music stops, and they stop dancing. She disengages herself from him and looks around. Suddenly She is intentionally cool*): We have moved too far from the others. You may take me—back, monsieur. (*She reaches for his arm, but Kerzhentsev takes her face roughly in his hands and kisses her. After he releases her, she says reproachfully*): What are you doing?

KERZHENTSEV: That's a kiss, my petite. Did it hurt?

(*He kisses her again, and as he lets her go she conveniently collapses on the lawn.*)

FOURTH ACTRESS: What are you waiting for? Stop torturing me. Take me—take what you will!

KERZHENTSEV: Merci. (*Tears off her beautiful wig, revealing thin, mousy hair.*) Je vous dis adieu, ma chère.

(*Humiliated, the Fourth Actress sobs. The Professor steps toward the platform, but Kerzhentsev with a leap confronts the First Actor.*)

Professor, let me answer this! Mr. Prosecuting Attorney, I have a confession to make. I admit I took pleasure in flattering those I despised, even in kissing those I hated. It made me feel superior: I felt freer and stronger than they were. But I never lied to myself. The more I lied to others, the more honest I became with myself. And if I open up the truth to you now, no matter how bad, it is certainly not to invite another superficial hypothesis. Yes, I mean you, Professor. What undoubtedly just now seemed to you a symptom of mental confusion was, in reality, abnormally normal.

PROFESSOR: I don't rule that out, but in what way "abnormally normal"?

KERZHENTSEV: Even as a child, I believed that the greatest work of nature is Reason, and consequently the greatest defect of the human organism is Emotion— please let me explain, Professor—I mean—that quality at the opposite pole from Reason, that boundless dark passion, masked by the word Love, which paralyzes the brain and sweeps a human being into a maelstrom of uncontrollable forces. And what is the embodiment of that dark spirit, Mr. Prosecuting Attorney? For me— it was Woman!

PROFESSOR (*Quickly*): Which one?

KERZHENTSEV: Any one! Each one! All! Starting with the unwashed Katya, right up to the last one, the Duchess de Cliche-Turomel. Because I began to understand

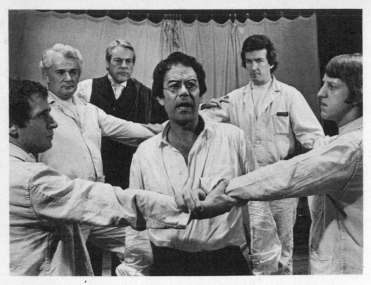

that every one—and this was really appalling—was in-
discriminately, without exception, longing only for a
sweaty, stinking bed, to couple, to mate, to grunt like
pigs and boars. (*He imitates a woman's voice*): "Oh,
Hamlet, speak no more! These words like daggers enter
in my ears." (*He speaks in his own voice and opens his
eyes, pointing into space*): "Save me, and hover o'er
me with your wings. You heavenly guards! What would
your gracious figure?" (*Back to woman's voice*): "Alas,
how is't with you?" (*He stops acting and turns on the
Actors*) : The Queen! Why is the Queen not here?

(*The First Actress, who has been trying to find all this
in her script, now gets up and frantically leafs through
to find her place. The pages fall from her hands and
scatter over the stage. There is general confusion.*)

You took away my sword, my knives, my forks, my
spoons, even the cups and glasses! All right. But why
did you take away my Queen, too? You . . . you . . .

(He runs forward. It isn't quite clear whether he wants to kill the Professor or the First Actor, who is trying to calm the First Actress. The Attendants grab Kerzhentsev roughly and hold him in a viselike grip.)

PROFESSOR *(With authority)*: Quiet! If you don't quiet down, we will use the strait-jacket, and we will stop this proceeding. *(Forces himself to calm down as well.)* You have made several mistakes, Mr. Kerzhentsev! You left out a number of scenes. The Queen has not yet entered.

(Kerzhentsev starts to laugh not at all like a madman, so that the Attendants instinctively ease their grip.)

KERZHENTSEV: Do you see, Mr. Prosecuting Attorney, how little it takes for our Professor to lock someone up among the madmen!

(The First Actor looks quizzically at the Professor, who simply shrugs.)

Do you think I don't know what happens next? Roxane has to enter first!

(A pause)

Forgive me the small deceit, gentlemen; it was essential if you are to understand the grand deceits.

(The Professor signals and the Attendants release Kerzhentsev. The First Actress attempts to rearrange the pages of her script, as the others hand them to her. The Attendants bring in a makeup table with a mirror.)

FIRST ACTOR *(Protectively to the First Actress)*: Is everything all right?
FIRST ACTRESS: Yes, thank you.
KERZHENTSEV: Allons! Cherchons la femme! Good morn-

ing, Alexey Konstantinovich. . . . (*Repeating the cue impatiently*): Good morning!

FIRST ACTOR (*Quickly putting a cold compress to his head*): Good morning.

KERZHENTSEV: Don't you feel well?

FIRST ACTOR: I drank a little bit again yesterday, and when I looked at myself in the mirror, it occurred to me that I was now ready to play Cyrano. There is a part in it for you, too.

KERZHENTSEV: Oh? What's the play all about?

FIRST ACTOR: Oh, the angelic Roxane loves the beautiful Christian for the sake of his soul, which she is discovering from his wonderful letters. Only, years after his death, she finds out that her ugly cousin, Cyrano, wrote them.

KERZHENTSEV: You mean she didn't know it all along?

FIRST ACTOR: Why would she pretend, then?

KERZHENTSEV: She wanted both the beautiful soul *and* the beautiful body. She didn't want to give up either one of them.

FIRST ACTOR (*Laughs*): That's quite like you, Kerzhentsev. . . . No, no, she really had no idea. That's why she went into the cloister after Christian's death.

KERZHENTSEV: And who is going to play this fairy-tale princess without the audience laughing her off the stage?

FIRST ACTOR: Allow me to introduce you to her. (*To the First Actress*): Mademoiselle, c'est mon ami Kerzhentsev, dont je vous ai raconté. (*She steps toward them. To Kerzhentsev*): Our new colleague, Tatyana Nikolayevna.

KERZHENTSEV (*Looks at her*): Dear God! (*Turns away as if offended.*) Professor! Gentlemen! I know when you cast a play you have to make concessions, but this is too much. She is playing the part of Tatyana? This one? Je proteste, je proteste!

(*First Actress turns away abruptly ready to leave.*)

FIRST ACTOR: Restez, madame, je vous en prie!

FIRST ACTRESS: Je ne peux pas. This is unbearable.

FIRST ACTOR: Mais c'est nécessaire . . . you must see it through! It's our duty!

PROFESSOR (*To Kerzhentsev*): You are an actor. You have imagination. Just pretend that she's your Tatyana. Tanya—moved back in time—but timeless, a Tanya now marked by suffering. Well?

KERZHENTSEV (*Kneeling in front of her and kissing her hand*): Tanya! My poor Tanya, forgive me. I only wanted the others to see you as you were on that particular winter morning when you didn't believe me and shattered my life. They can't possibly imagine how beautiful you were, how your eyes laughed, when I thought they'd cry. And if your face has now become as pale as ashes, and the skin of your hand no more than a glove, then the fault is mine, and I am a murderer twice over. (*Stops talking suddenly.*)

PROFESSOR (*After a pause, to the First Actor*): I believe this pause belongs to your next scene.

(*First Actress draws her hand away from Kerzhentsev and slowly moves away.*)

KERZHENTSEV: Dear God!

FIRST ACTOR: Kerzhentsev!

KERZHENTSEV (*Raising his head. Suddenly he becomes a different man, quiet and modest*): Yes?

FIRST ACTOR: What's the matter with you?

KERZHENTSEV: What is the matter with me?

FIRST ACTOR: Why don't you speak?

KERZHENTSEV: What shall I say?

FIRST ACTOR: Your lines.

KERZHENTSEV: What lines?

FIRST ACTOR: Are you asleep, or are you drunk? You broke off in the middle of Christian's speech.

KERZHENTSEV (*Getting control of himself*): Excuse me, Alexey Konstantinovich. I don't feel well.

FIRST ACTOR (*Placing his hand on Kerzhentsev's forehead*): You have a fever.

KERZHENTSEV: Yes.

FIRST ACTOR: Go and lie down, mon frère. I'll stand in for you in the rehearsal. Anyhow, Cyrano and Christian are two sides of the same coin.

KERZHENTSEV: Yes . . .

FIRST ACTOR: He should go home. It's exactly as in Rostand's play, Tatyana Nikolayevna. There too you lose your man before he can say what you want to hear from him—go, Kerzhentsev, get well for your Roxane.

(*Tries to send Kerzhentsev away, but he resists.*)

KERZHENTSEV: No. The line I wrote hasn't been said yet.

PROFESSOR: He means your line, madame.

FIRST ACTRESS (*Getting control of herself*) : Get well soon, my dear Anton Ignatyevich . . .

KERZHENTSEV (*Repeats the sentence as if it were in code*) : Get well soon, my dear Anton Ignatyevich . . . (*He looks upward.*) Dear God! Why did you first make me evil and then send me this woman? Why didn't you decide one way or the other? . . . Or are you sending her to me to destroy the evil in me? If so, then you really are all-knowing. Her first glance made me a child again, innocent and pure. . . . And her voice . . . "Get well soon, my dear Anton Ignatyevich." . . . Father, if she says yes to me, then I'm ready for any sacrifice, because in having her I'll have everything. And if you're really all-powerful, then make it so that today, the fifth of January, at the Petersburg railway station, I can buy roses for her.

SECOND ACTRESS (*With a basket of artificial roses*): Roses! Fresh roses! Buy roses!

KERZHENTSEV (*Gratefully looking up to heaven*): Thank you! How much?

SECOND ACTRESS: One rose, one ruble, sir. They came on a boat from Holland.

KERZHENTSEV: I don't want to know how much they cost, just how many you have.

SECOND ACTRESS: Fifty, sir.

KERZHENTSEV: Couldn't I have a hundred?

SECOND ACTRESS: Oh no, sir! They cost one ruble.

(*He gives her a banknote, pushes her away, and turns to the Fourth Actor.*)

KERZHENTSEV: Conductor: is this the only train to Moscow?

FOURTH ACTOR: The only one, Your Excellency.

KERZHENTSEV: The only sleeping car?

FOURTH ACTOR: The only one, Your Excellency.

KERZHENTSEV: How many minutes do we have left?

FOURTH ACTOR: Five, Your Exce—

KERZHENTSEV: Listen! I'm waiting here for a lady. Obviously, she'll be here only at the last moment. (*He gives him a banknote.*) I want to speak to her for ten minutes, do you understand?

FOURTH ACTOR: Excuse me, Your Excellency, but that's not . . .

KERZHENTSEV (*Gives him another banknote*): Five minutes!

FOURTH ACTOR: Very well, Your Excel—

THIRD ACTOR (*Monocled, accompanied by the Third Actress*): Excuse me, sir, have I the honor of addressing Mr. Kerzhentsev?

KERZHENTSEV (*Absentminded*): Yes.

THIRD ACTOR: Major Count Byelitsky and wife. We are among your many admirers.

THIRD ACTRESS: I've seen *Cyrano* three times just because of your Christian!

KERZHENTSEV: Thank you. Can I do anything else for you?

THIRD ACTOR (*Stammering*): You obviously don't understand. . . . I am Major Count Byelitsky—

KERZHENTSEV (*Turning away from them and running toward the First Actress*): Tatyana Nikolayevna!

THIRD ACTRESS: Roxane! Oh, forgive us, we had no way of knowing . . . (*Turning excitedly to the Third Actor*): Oh, then it *is* true!

FIRST ACTRESS (*In traveling coat, carrying a small valise*): Anton Ignatyevich! What a coincidence! Are you traveling to Moscow? That's wonderful!

KERZHENTSEV: One word from you will be enough for me to go to the ends of the earth.

FIRST ACTRESS (*Laughs*): Ah, funny . . . as always. *(Sees the flowers.)* Forgive me. I don't want to keep you . . .

KERZHENTSEV: Keep me? From whom?

FIRST ACTRESS: You came to say goodbye to someone.

KERZHENTSEV: No, I came to say hello to someone.

FIRST ACTRESS: Then you're on the wrong platform. The train leaves for Moscow from here.

KERZHENTSEV: I came to say hello to you, Tatyana Nikolayevna!

FIRST ACTRESS: But I'm leaving!

KERZHENTSEV: And I am celebrating your arrival.

FIRST ACTRESS: You *are* an amusing man, Anton Ignatyevich. God will keep you till we meet again. Oh, I see I made it just in time. Take care!

KERZHENTSEV (*Stops her*): Don't worry. We still have five minutes.

FIRST ACTRESS (*Looking at the clock*): But . . .

KERZHENTSEV: I bribed the conductor.

FIRST ACTRESS: But why?

KERZHENTSEV: Because I want to talk to you.

FIRST ACTRESS: You talk to me every day.

KERZHENTSEV: Words someone else wrote.

FIRST ACTRESS: Do you mean Rostand or Cyrano?

KERZHENTSEV: The devil with him! I'm not Christian, Tatyana Nikolayevna. I'm Anton Ignatyevich Kerzhentsev! I have a soul, too.

FIRST ACTRESS: My dear, now I really don't understand you! I have the feeling . . .

KERZHENTSEV: You're mistaken, if you have the feeling I'm joking.

FIRST ACTRESS: No, I don't have . . .

KERZHENTSEV: I stopped joking exactly fifty-five days ago.

FIRST ACTRESS: That is—amazing. But why do you tell me this?

KERZHENTSEV: Fifty-five days—doesn't that tell you anything?

FIRST ACTRESS: What should it tell me?

KERZHENTSEV: We have known each other—just fifty-five days!

FIRST ACTRESS (*Laughs again*): And along with everything else, you're also very imaginative. It was lovely, but I really must go now. My parents expect me tomorrow.

KERZHENTSEV (*Whispers*): Tanya. (*She turns back to him.*) Yes . . . Tanya! Tell your parents that a man who has never asked anyone for anything, tonight asked you to marry him.

(*He sees that she's embarrassed, and he raises his arms to embrace her, but she begins to laugh with relief. He stares at her, wordlessly. A Musician gives the signal that the train is ready to leave.*)

FIRST ACTRESS (*Still laughing*): Oh, forgive me please— the roses—and that voice . . . I almost believed you.

KERZHENTSEV (*With difficulty*): Almost? You almost . . .

FIRST ACTRESS: Your eyes gave you away. Adieu.

KERZHENTSEV (*Forcing a smile*): My eyes? How amusing. Adieu. (*She leaves quickly. He looks upward.*) Did I hear You say—hell? Then Thy will be done. But even if I could forgive her her laughter, I will never forgive her my smile. Fear my smile from now on, Tatyana Nikolayevna! Ah, get me something to drink! (*An Attendant hurries to him with a cup he has filled from a water pitcher. Kerzhentsev drinks, and spits the liquid out.*) What did you give me, you rascal?

ATTENDANT: Water.

PROFESSOR: I am sorry, Mr. Kerzhentsev. He made a mistake. This isn't your waiter. Let me get you a more experienced one.

(*At the Professor's signal, the Second Actor quickly puts on an apron and takes over.*)

SECOND ACTOR: Would you care to try this one, Your Excellency? (*He hands him the same cup.*)

KERZHENTSEV (*Takes a sip and rolls it appreciatively over his tongue. Takes a larger sip, then empties the cup with a connoisseur's acknowledgment*): Like the fires of hell!

SECOND ACTOR: Old vodka from Tula. Double distilled especially for us.

KERZHENTSEV: More! That's exactly what I needed. Here you are! (*Throws him a ruble.*)

SECOND ACTOR: God bless you, Your Excellency.

KERZHENTSEV: How long have you been a waiter?

SECOND ACTOR: Forty years, Your Excellency.

KERZHENTSEV (*Drinks his cup down*): That's good! Ah, but it didn't warm my soul. What do you have to warm my soul?

SECOND ACTOR: That depends on what chills your soul, Your Excellency.

KERZHENTSEV: Humiliation.

SECOND ACTOR: You can't drown humiliation, Your Excellency, you can only pay it back.

KERZHENTSEV: Oh? And with what? Can you tell me that too?

SECOND ACTOR: I think Your Excellency knows.

KERZHENTSEV: I want to hear it from you!

SECOND ACTOR: With—revenge.

KERZHENTSEV: You said that, not I! Good night Alexey Konstantinovich! Say good night to Tatyana Nikolayevna.

FIRST ACTOR: What? Aren't you going to take her home?

KERZHENTSEV: I thought you were.

FIRST ACTOR: Why me?

KERZHENTSEV: I thought you were fond of her.

FIRST ACTOR: That's not important. For all of Petersburg, there's only one ideal couple—she and you!

KERZHENTSEV: You should know better than anyone, that couple exists only behind the footlights.

FIRST ACTOR: But I myself had the feeling you fell in love with her.

KERZHENTSEV: I?

FIRST ACTOR: I even thought that you fell in love for the first time in your life. Until that moment it seemed to me that it was the only feeling denied you. That's why I wanted you to have this experience.

KERZHENTSEV: *You* wanted me to have this experience?

FIRST ACTOR: Is it so strange for me to want you to be happy?

KERZHENTSEV: But you could be happy with her yourself.

FIRST ACTOR (*Taking another cup*): For yourself, you can only die. For love, you need at least two.

KERZHENTSEV: But what if she wants to be happy only with you?

FIRST ACTOR: Nonsense! No, that's nonsense, Anton. Good night. Sleep well.

KERZHENTSEV: Alexey Konstantinovich! Why don't you believe me?

FIRST ACTOR: Why should I? She's never even said one word—

KERZHENTSEV: Allow me to remind you, it's not usually the woman who speaks first. Why don't you talk to her?

FIRST ACTOR: No, no! I would never stand in your way.

KERZHENTSEV: Then let me tell you that I love Tatyana Nikolayevna only as Christian. When the curtain comes down, she is just another actress.

FIRST ACTOR: How can that be possible, Anton?

KERZHENTSEV: I don't know.

FIRST ACTOR: You can't deny she's the most exquisite being in all Petersburg.

KERZHENTSEV: That's why only you deserve her.

FIRST ACTOR: Poor Kerzhentsev. You don't know what you're giving up.

KERZHENTSEV: Poor Savelyov, you *should* know!

FIRST ACTRESS (*Enters*): Gentlemen, may I seek refuge with you? Or is this a private conversation . . . ?

KERZHENTSEV: Not at all, Tatyana Nikolayevna. Alexey Konstantinovich never misses a chance to talk theatre.

FIRST ACTRESS: Yes, that's been my experience, too.

KERZHENTSEV: Has someone upset you?

FIRST ACTRESS: Everyone here has obviously made a wager who will take me home. I'm afraid it will all end in a scandal, and I don't know how to prevent it.

KERZHENTSEV: Alexey Konstantinovich is just trying to decide whether or not to accompany you himself—after all, he is our director.

FIRST ACTOR (*To First Actress*): But only if you agree. Tatyana—the same courtesy could be provided as well by—

FIRST ACTRESS (*Cutting him short with a smile*): Pourquoi pas? I accept with pleasure. (*Taking First Actor's arm*): Good night, Anton Ignatyevich.

FIRST ACTOR (*Embarrassed, to Kerzhentsev*): Well . . . aren't you coming, too? You wanted to . . . didn't you . . . ?

KERZHENTSEV: No, I think I'll stay a little longer. Good night. (*First Actor and First Actress leave.*) Good night! Sleep well—and the devil take you both—preferably together!

PROFESSOR: What does this mean, Mr. Kerzhentsev? You hand over the woman you love to someone else? Why do I say "hand over"—you brought them closer together, closer than the friendliest fate could have done! What kind of revenge is that?

KERZHENTSEV: An ingenious revenge, Professor! And just as cruel as her laughter at the railway station. She needed him as a measure, to understand what she had lost. She needed to experience his complacency and indecision, his constant drunkenness, his sentimentality, his eternal headaches, his incapacity to love or be loved. She also needed—and this image gave me a strange exhilaration—to experience his slack embraces, to be reminded how differently she was embraced only an hour before by Anton Ignatyevich Kerzhentsev, and on a stage. And I was waiting like an evil demon for her to admit her defeat.

PROFESSOR: And then you would forgive her?

KERZHENTSEV: No! I don't forgive, Professor. I never forgive.

PROFESSOR: Then what did you have in mind?

KERZHENTSEV: Let her go ahead with her script, Professor. Let her say what she has to say, and I will do what I have prepared myself to do all these long weeks and months. I saw this moment very clearly even before it actually happened: We are standing next to each other, holding hands, we bow, only the two of us. When the last curtain falls, she whispers to me, "Anton Ignatyevich, I have to tell you something . . ."

FIRST ACTRESS (*At a signal from the Professor, she takes Kerzhentsev's hand and repeats*): "Anton Ignatyevich, I have to tell you something."

KERZHENTSEV (*As in a trance*): "I have to apologize to you . . ."

FIRST ACTRESS: "I have to apologize to you . . ."

KERZHENTSEV: "I thought you were a vain egotist . . ."

FIRST ACTRESS: "I thought you were a vain egotist . . ."

KERZHENTSEV: "But I was wrong . . ."

FIRST ACTRESS: "But I was wrong . . ."

KERZHENTSEV: "I realize that I love you, only you . . ."

—and now, Professor, listen very carefully. She: "I realize that I love you, only you . . ." And I? (*Crosses his arms as he did before the corpse of his father and laughs right into her face.)*

PROFESSOR (*Stopping him*): But she didn't say that!

KERZHENTSEV (*Stops laughing, wakes as if from a trance*): What? Oh, yes! She said it. Nearly word for word!

PROFESSOR: Except for the last sentence.

KERZHENTSEV: That's a lie!

PROFESSOR: Mr. Kerzhentsev! (*Showing him the script*): We are going by your text. This is your text, isn't it?

KERZHENTSEV (*Looks at the script as if for the first time*): Yes, Yes . . .

PROFESSOR (*To the First Actress*): May I ask you to do it again, please?

KERZHENTSEV (*In a dead voice*): Yes . . .

FIRST ACTRESS: "Anton Ignatyevich, I have to tell you something. I have to apologize to you. I thought you were a vain egotist but I was wrong. I realize that I have you and only you to thank for my happiness. And I want you to know that."

KERZHENTSEV: Your happiness?

FIRST ACTOR (*Coming to them and embracing them both*): Kerzhentsev, today Tanya said yes!

KERZHENTSEV: Yes?

FIRST ACTOR: Yes. Yes. Yes. Yes. Yes! In return for all the roles I gave to you, you've given me the most beautiful one. (*He embraces First Actress.*) Our happiness is your doing, and that's why you're the only one who can give my future wife to me at the altar.

(First Actor takes both their hands and joins them. The orchestra plays the Wedding March. All walk in pairs behind Kerzhentsev and First Actress, who wears a white veil.)

KERZHENTSEV: Again, she had betrayed me. Again! It wasn't enough that she had turned me down! She had to marry a man who in nothing—in nothing!—can be compared with me! Her face is beautiful—without a care—radiant: as if she weren't going to the altar with a miserable clown, but as if she were going with me, as all of Petersburg expected. Another irony, a public slap in the face. A betrayal! And I will take a revenge as terrible as it deserves!

PROFESSOR (*Interrupts the music*): Wouldn't you like to rest, Mr. Kerzhentsev?

KERZHENTSEV (*As if he hadn't heard*): I'm going to make him repulsive to her! If she doesn't yet know who he is, I'll introduce him to her! I'll prove to her that she doesn't mean that much (*Snaps his fingers*)—to him. Not so much.

PROFESSOR: How will you do that? Don't forget, he loves her.

KERZHENTSEV: Yes, but he believes me—he believes my eyes! (*He throws off his jacket, opens his shirt, and runs his fingers through his hair.*) Savelyov!

FIRST ACTOR (*Going to Kerzhentsev*) : Anton, what is it —what's the matter with you?

KERZHENTSEV: I don't know. It's all meaningless.

FIRST ACTOR: Poor Kerzhentsev! Tell me, what can I do for you?

KERZHENTSEV: Kill me!

FIRST ACTOR: But we all need you. Your eyes give people reassurance and happiness.

KERZHENTSEV: I hate people.

FIRST ACTOR: I know what will make you feel better. I was going to play Hamlet again in our new production. I want you to play him.

KERZHENTSEV: I hate the theatre. Let me go!

FIRST ACTOR: Anton, come home with me. Tanya will take care of you. Believe me, Tanya knows how to take care of all sorrows.

KERZHENTSEV: Not mine.

FIRST ACTOR: Fall in love, Kerzhentsev! Why don't you fall in love? Every human being needs someone to live for.

KERZHENTSEV: I don't want to live. I don't like myself.

FIRST ACTOR: Then what do you want, my friend?

KERZHENTSEV: I want to get drunk. You taught me how. You come with me.

FIRST ACTOR: You know, I don't drink anymore.

KERZHENTSEV: I'll show you how again.

FIRST ACTOR: No, I promised Tanya to spend this evening with her.

KERZHENTSEV: Yes . . . yes, I understand. (*Turns away from him.*)

FIRST ACTOR: We'll do it tomorrow.

KERZHENTSEV (*Smiling sadly*): Tomorrow? Who knows about tomorrow? Adieu. Thank you for doing everything you could for me. (*He starts to leave.*)

FIRST ACTOR (*Suddenly deciding*): Wait! I'll go with you.

(*At once, the stage is transformed into a tavern. A Gypsy band is playing, and the First Actor, already drunk, drinks and dances with two Gypsy girls.*)

KERZHENTSEV (*Holding a cup to the First Actor's lips*):
Drink, Savelyov, drink! Drink to your happiness!

FIRST ACTOR (*Drunk*): Yes. I'm happy! I'm a happy
man, do you hear, Kerzhentsev? Do you hear? I'm a
happy man!

(*The Gypsies gather around, applauding and toasting
him.*)

KERZHENTSEV (*Turning to the Second Actress*): You
hear, Roma? You'd better listen to him. Maybe you'll
hear something you haven't heard from me.

FIRST ACTOR: Yes, I love, Kerzhentsev! I, who was so
convinced that love was nothing more than poetry true
only for a passing moment, and only in the theatre
through the Art of the Actor. Now I *understand* that
one can *play* only a tiny fraction of what love really is.
Why are you fighting it? What do you expect to gain
by it?

KERZHENTSEV: What you have lost: freedom.

FIRST ACTOR: Freedom can only be lost when there's not
enough love. A great enough love gives freedom wings.

KERZHENTSEV: Then you are freer than I am?

FIRST ACTOR (*Shouts at the top of his voice*): I'm the
freest human being in the world because I have more
love than any of you.

KERZHENTSEV: Hear that, Roma? Maybe he'll give you
what I can't afford.

SECOND ACTRESS (*Sits on First Actor's lap*): Love me,
Your Excellency! Love little Roma, who wants love so
much!

FIRST ACTOR: Why not? God, why not? I have so much
love, there's enough for you, too.

KERZHENTSEV: Love is not everything, Savelyov. Roma
wants more.

FIRST ACTOR (*Taking money from his pocket*): Money? Here! Take it! Take it! I want you to be as happy as I am.

KERZHENTSEV: Then give her a wedding ring.

SECOND ACTRESS: Yes. Yes. Give little Roma a beautiful big ring!

FIRST ACTOR: Why not? (*Takes ring from his finger.*) Take mine!

KERZHENTSEV: Yours will be too big for her, Alexey. Give her your wife's wedding ring.

FIRST ACTOR (*To Second Actress*): If you think it'll bring you luck, you shall have it. Tanya will love me even without a ring. Hey, Gypsy!

FOURTH ACTOR: Your Excellency?

FIRST ACTOR: Go to this address, say to the maid: "The master orders Tatyana Nikolayevna to send him her ring."

KERZHENTSEV: Repeat that!

FOURTH ACTOR: The master orders Tatyana Nikolayevna to send him the ring.

FIRST ACTOR: *Her* ring! Her wedding ring!

FOURTH ACTOR: Hers! Her wedding ring! And if she doesn't believe me?

KERZHENTSEV: Then tell her to bring it herself.

(*Laughter*)

Do you understand?

FOURTH ACTOR: I understand. But I *don't* understand why Your Excellency doesn't just cut his throat right away.

(*Laughter*)

FIRST ACTOR: Come to me, Roma. And you, Gypsies, sing! Sing to us of the happiness of a happy people!

(*The Gypsies and Musicians gather around them and sing a slow Gypsy romance.*)

KERZHENTSEV (*To the Professor*): Once, in the autumn, Professor, in the park, I watched a little girl bundled up in a warm coat trying to get near a tiny little dog who had fearfully pulled in his tail. Suddently she got frightened, turned, and ran and hid her face in her nurse's lap. The dog blinked fearfully, and the nurse smiled stupidly and said—more to me than anyone else, I don't know why—"Don't be frightened." Two or three times, "Don't be frightened." Seeing this scene under the clear fall sun, I had a strange feeling that all of my cold lies came from some separate, foreign world: they were so little, the girl and the dog, they were so frightened of each other in such a funny way—and there was so much wisdom in that—as if the solution of all the riddles of life was hidden just there. I don't know why I'm telling you this silly and irrelevant story. Yes, yes . . . probably I thought of that story again during the night while I was waiting for Tatyana to see her damned happiness crumble to dust! I remember I said to myself: You must think everything through one more time . . . I just repeated that sentence mechanically over and over again until it was too late.

FIRST ACTRESS (*Coming quickly onto the platform accompanied by the Fourth Actor*): Anton Ignatyevich?!

KERZHENTSEV: Tatyana Nikolayevna, for God's sake.

FIRST ACTRESS: What's the matter with Alexey? Where is my husband?

KERZHENTSEV: For the sake of our friendship . . . Go home!

FIRST ACTRESS: What happened to him?

KERZHENTSEV: Nothing. I swear, nothing. Just what happens to any man sometimes, even the most beloved.

FIRST ACTRESS: I want to see him!

KERZHENTSEV: I promise you, I'll bring him safely home. Don't go to him!

FIRST ACTRESS: I'm his wife. He sent for me.

KERZHENTSEV: He's drunk.

FIRST ACTRESS: Then he needs me even more.

KERZHENTSEV: If that's what you want!

(*Kerzhentsev claps his hands; the Gypsies stop singing and scatter silently. The First Actor is discovered in an embrace with the Second Actress.*)

FIRST ACTOR (*To Second Actress*): Are you happy, my darling?

FIRST ACTRESS (*Answering for the Second Actress*): Yes, Aljoscha. And you?

FIRST ACTOR (*Seeing her*): Tanya! My Tanya! (*He slides to her on his knees and embraces her legs.*) Oh, dear God, I am happy.

FIRST ACTRESS: I brought my ring, to whom shall I give it? To her?

SECOND ACTRESS (*Frightened*): No. No.

FIRST ACTRESS: Don't be afraid. Take it! What he wants, I want, and if your happiness is his happiness, it is mine as well. (*She takes her wedding ring off and gives it to the Second Actress.*)

SECOND ACTRESS: No! (*She runs away.*)

FIRST ACTOR: I love you, Tanya. (*He passes out.*)

FIRST ACTRESS: And I love you. (*To the others*): Help him to the coach, please.

(*They lift him to their shoulders and carry him off.*)

KERZHENTSEV: No! It cannot be!

FIRST ACTRESS: What cannot be?

KERZHENTSEV: Is this you? You? To whom the best men of Petersburg offered their souls?

FIRST ACTRESS: I wasn't aware of that.

KERZHENTSEV: The world has never seen a just woman.

FIRST ACTRESS: How am I unjust?

KERZHENTSEV: To whom do you give your love? To a drunken animal?

FIRST ACTRESS: Yes, to him!

KERZHENTSEV: To a man who trades you for the first Gypsy who comes along?

FIRST ACTRESS: Yes, to him!

KERZHENTSEV: To a man who doesn't even know the secret meaning of life, who doesn't even know the difference between the truth and a lie. Who should know better than you what a bad artist he is!

FIRST ACTRESS: Who should know better than I what a good man he is!

KERZHENTSEV: A good man? Who is good in this miserable world? What is good and what is bad? A smile can be bad—a murder can be good.

FIRST ACTRESS: For me, it is enough to serve a good human being.

KERZHENTSEV: He destroyed you, and I will never forgive him.

FIRST ACTRESS: I believe there's something else you can't forgive him, Anton Ignatyevich.

KERZHENTSEV: What?

FIRST ACTRESS: That he is my husband and that I love him. (*Kerzhentsev cringes.*) And I tell you plainly, if he didn't like you so much . . .

KERZHENTSEV (*With difficulty*): Finish it.

FIRST ACTRESS: . . . I wouldn't waste another word on you.

(*She leaves. Kerzhentsev reaches out, and the Second Actor hands him a cup.*)

SECOND ACTOR: You can't drown humiliation in vodka. You can only pay it back, Your Excellency.

KERZHENTSEV: But with what?

SECOND ACTOR: You know.

KERZHENTSEV: I want to hear it again.

SECOND ACTOR: With revenge.

KERZHENTSEV: But what kind of revenge? Every trap I set slams shut behind me and I'm locked inside while she parades in front of me with her prize.

SECOND ACTOR: Then take her prize away from her!

KERZHENTSEV: What? (*He almost begins to laugh; but breaks off, turns to the First Actress—who has returned to her chair—as if to say something unusually witty*): Tatyana Nikolayevna, you really do love your husband. Good . . . Then I'll simply kill him.

(*The First Actress faints. The Professor and the others rush to help her.*)

Act II

A short time later. The First Actress, already seated, responds to the questioning glance of the Professor with a nod. He claps his hands, and an Attendant draws the curtain. Kerzhentsev is seated in a chair, guarded by two Attendants. His eyes are closed and his head bent against his shoulder.

PROFESSOR: What's the matter with him?

ATTENDANT: He's asleep, Your Excellency.

PROFESSOR (*Goes to the platform and professionally draws Kerzhentsev's eyelid up*): He is! He's asleep.

KERZHENTSEV (*Suddenly opening his eyes. Brightly*): Intermission over?

PROFESSOR (*Stunned*): Yes . . . Do you want to continue?

KERZHENTSEV: Only Death can interrupt the play, Professor—or the Stage Director. So—what do you think of it so far? How is it going?

(*General applause*)

PROFESSOR: I beg your pardon?

KERZHENTSEV: Never mind . . .

PROFESSOR (*To the Actors*): Will you please . . .

KERZHENTSEV (*Turns to the others*): I thank you, my

friends . . . for giving so much truth to insignificant characters. (*Glancing at Professor*): Too bad we don't have an audience to appreciate it. (*Pointing at Professor*):
"What's Hecuba to him, or he to Hecuba,
That he should weep for her? What would he do,
Had he the motive and the cue for passion
That I have?"
Why don't we all go for a drink? (*He turns to Attendant; as if giving him an order*): Reserve a table at the Theatre Club in my name! Fear not, I'm staying here with you. Well, then! Let's see . . . (*He jumps up.*) Flourish!

(*The Musicians, surprised, play somewhat badly.*)

One, Alexey Savelyov had to be killed. Two! Tatyana Nikolayevna had to *know* that I killed him. Three! He had to be killed in such a way that I could not be convicted. If only to prevent her from another triumph over me. I have to admit, gentlemen: I loved life too much. It's interesting, I even loved the cruel games it plays. And I loved myself, the strength of my muscles, the power of my lucid, precise mind. Of all the men I've ever met, I was the only one I honestly appreciated. Should I risk depriving myself of the possibility of experiencing life in its total richness and depth? Why should I hand myself over to a house of correction or into the uncouth hands of the executioner? As an artist too—and certainly I was a brighter artist than Savelyov —I intended to gain further laurels. Therefore, the deed had to be done without consequent punishment. Do you understand?

PROFESSOR: We understand, Mr. Kerzhentsev, but it's still not clear how you expected to accomplish that.

KERZHENTSEV: That wasn't clear to me, either. Being a former medical doctor, I said to myself there are at least a thousand ways to kill a patient. True, Professor?

PROFESSOR: For instance?

KERZHENTSEV: For instance . . . (*With a wink*): by injecting a really repulsive, incurable disease into his veins. Let's assume that, Professor.

PROFESSOR: All right, let's *assume* that.

KERZHENTSEV: But I dismissed it. It would take too long and it seemed—crude—and somehow—too unreasonable. Besides, there was the danger that Tatyana Nikolayevna would get a certain consolation from taking care of her husband. No! His death had to hit her like a bolt of lightning, and she had to see me do it.

PROFESSOR: But didn't this present an insoluble problem for you?

KERZHENTSEV: Only cowards fear obstacles. Strong natures like mine are attracted by them, inspired. I admit it took desperately long, but at last I got help from an ally.

PROFESSOR: From whom?

KERZHENTSEV (*Gets up, points into space, eyes wide*): "Save me, and hover o'er me with your wings,
You heavenly guards! What would your gracious figure?"

FIRST ACTRESS (*Approaching him*): "Alas, how is't with you,
That you do bend your eye on vacancy
And with the incorporal air do hold discourse?
Forth at your eyes your spirits wildly peep;
And, as the sleeping soldiers in the alarm,
Your bedded hairs, like life in excrements,
Start up and stand on end. O gentle son,
Upon the heat and flame of thy distemper
Sprinkle cool patience. Whereon do you look?"

KERZHENTSEV:

"Why, look you there! look, how it steals away!
My father, in his habit as he lived!"

FIRST ACTRESS:

"This is the very coinage of your brain:
This bodiless creation ecstasy
Is very cunning in."

KERZHENTSEV:

                                        "Ecstasy!
My pulse, as yours, doth temperately keep time,
And makes as healthful music: it is not madness
That I have utter'd: bring me to the test,
And I the matter will re-word, which madness
Would gambol from. Mother, for love of grace,
Lay not that flattering unction to your soul,
That not your trespass but my madness speaks."

FIRST ACTRESS:

"O Hamlet, thou hast cleft my heart in twain."

KERZHENTSEV:

"Oh, throw away the worser part of it,
And live the purer with the other half."

FIRST ACTRESS:

"What shall I do?"

KERZHENTSEV:

"Not this, by no means, that I bid you do:
Let the bloat king tempt you again to bed;
Pinch wanton on your cheek, call you his mouse;
And let him, for a pair of reechy kisses,
Or paddling in your neck with his damn'd fingers,
Make you to ravel all this matter out,
That I essentially am not in madness,
But mad in craft. For who . . ." (*He falls silent.*)

FIRST ACTOR (*Prompting*):

"For who, that's but a queen . . ."

(*Kerzhentsev doesn't respond. Louder*) :
"For who, that's but a queen, fair, sober, wise,
Would . . ."

KERZHENTSEV (*Slowly*):
"For who, that's but a queen, fair, sober, wise,
Would from a paddock, from a bat, a gib,
Such dear concernings hide?" (*Silent again.*)

FIRST ACTOR: Anton, what's the matter with you? Don't you know the text?

KERZHENTSEV: Of course I know it. Do you want to hear it?

FIRST ACTOR: Yes, I would like to, of course.

KERZHENTSEV (*Staring at him*):
"But come; gentlemen, swear
Here, as before, never, so help you mercy,
How strange or odd soe'er I bear myself,
To put an antic disposition on . . .
That you, at such times seeing me, never shall give out,
    to note
That you know aught of me: this not to do.
Swear."

FIRST ACTOR: You've already said this speech today.

KERZHENTSEV: What do you mean?

FIRST ACTOR: That's from the first act and we're doing the third act now . . . the dialogue with the Queen after the murder of Polonius.

KERZHENTSEV: Oh, I'm sorry, I got confused—Polonius —that's you, of course, and you're still alive.

FIRST ACTOR: Are you ill again? (*Puts his arm around him.*) Maybe you're overtired, mon frère. Go, take a rest. I'll rehearse for you.

KERZHENTSEV (*Drops the Hamlet cape*): Rehearse, Savelyov! And I will rehearse what chance—the greatest ally of all geniuses—just whispered to me. Why should a sane lunatic from Elsinore not take revenge in *Petersburg*, as well? Now, as a medical man—who never bothered to practice—I knew that in the wide field of psychopathology there are vast territories still uncharted, that there is sufficient room left for fantasy and subjective judgment. I hope I don't offend you too much, Professor—or your colleagues—if I say I knew I could put my fate safely in your hands. I knew I could convince you I was insane.

PROFESSOR: I admit, compared with other disciplines, we are far behind, Mr. Kerzhentsev, but not so far that we wouldn't be able to see through an obvious simulation.

KERZHENTSEV: In what way obvious, Professor? You always keep forgetting you're actually speaking with a colleague. The first thing you had to take into account was—Inherited Tendencies. Am I right?

PROFESSOR: Well . . . Yes . . .

KERZHENTSEV: Well then—my father was a drunkard. Isn't that marvelous? His brother died, as they say so elegantly, in a sanatorium for the melancholically inclined. My dear departed sister suffered from epilepsy, fortunately for us. Enough?

PROFESSOR: I should say so.

KERZHENTSEV: And what about me? What about my Arrogance—which between us is simply a sign of mental superiority—couldn't it be interpreted as a Malignant Case of Misanthropy? What about my healthy Asceticism? Isn't there some sort of link *there* to my Artistic Egocentric Tendencies, making for Monomania and an obsession with an idée fixe?

PROFESSOR: All of that wouldn't be . . .

KERZHENTSEV: . . . wouldn't be enough, I know, but with it we establish the statics of madness. Now, it was

just a question of the dynamics. To the sketch provided by nature, only two or three ingenious strokes had to be added, and the picture was complete. Haven't I given you enough demonstrations of my rare talent for histrionics?

PROFESSOR: Up to this point, even though you wanted to shock, you've stayed within the framework of the familiar, so to speak. But have you considered, Mr. Kerzhentsev, that in the experiment you are now daring to make, there is tremendous danger?

KERZHENTSEV (*Smiles*): Are you trying to say that a man who starts a fire in a cellar full of high explosives is in much less danger than a man who admits a breath of madness into his brain?

PROFESSOR: Approximately.

KERZHENTSEV: I had an unconquerable defense against that danger.

PROFESSOR: What?

KERZHENTSEV: My intellect: cold and certain as a rapier,

firm in my grip. Obedient. My slave, my power, my only possession. How I loved my intellect, and still love it! Yet I tested it, and I am testing it again, right now, for your sake as well as for mine.

(*Music, a Mazurka; everyone dances. Kerzhentsev takes a top hat and a scarf from an Attendant and instantly hands it to another Attendant.*)

THIRD ACTOR (*Exuberantly*): Anton Ignatyevich! Maestro, quel honneur! Thank God!

THIRD ACTRESS: Anton Ignatyevich! My little dove! Quel plaisir! We were afraid that you, too, were going to let us down.

KERZHENTSEV: Me, too?

THIRD ACTRESS: Just imagine, Tatyana Nikolayevna and Alexey Konstantinovich begged off at the last moment. Est-ce que ce n'est pas triste? Come, my dear, everyone is waiting for you.

(*She takes him by the arm and leads him to the table, which has been set by the Attendants. Elegant guests take their places. The host stands at the head of the table.*)

Our guests wanted to see Tatyana Nikolayevna so much. And you, of course. You're not cross, are you, that we link you two together? We're simply your audience enchanted by the magic of the stage. Whether you're cross or not, I'll tell you in confidence: I will never understand why you didn't marry her. Good God, why are you so pale?

KERZHENTSEV (*Looks up into space*): If I am pale, it's because I want to be. Tatyana didn't come! That means that now is the time to make the test, because if there is anyone in the world who couldn't be deceived by it, it's her.

THIRD ACTRESS (*Following Kerzhentsev's gaze*): What? What are you looking at, Anton Ignatyevich?

KERZHENTSEV: I? Do I look?

THIRD ACTRESS: You keep looking—up.

KERZHENTSEV: Yes? Then I must have seen somebody there.

THIRD ACTRESS: Oh, you're a naughty boy! (*She teasingly shakes her finger at him.*) With you actors one never knows what's next. That's what's so exciting about the theatre.

THIRD ACTOR (*Clapping his hands*): Silence! S'il vous plaît! (*The Mazurka comes to a stop. Festively*): Mesdames, messieurs! We have the honor to welcome to our circle a most illustrious guest—and I may say—the star of the Petersburg Theatre, our beloved—I may say, if I include our wives too, their beloved, yes, loved, maestro, Anton Ignatyevich Kerzhentsev. (*All applaud ecstatically, but Kerzhentsev stands immobile, absently gazing into space.*) Anton Ignatyevich has been so kind as to honor us with his presence and he has graciously agreed to preface our dinner with—I may say—a jewel of lyric poetry, a sonnet by Petrarch, which he has memorized just for us. My dear Anton Ignatyevich, we are all yours.

(*Kerzhentsev turns to the Professor, winks significantly at him, then looks out into space again. There is a pause.*)

THIRD ACTOR (*Coughs*): Anton Ignatyevich—!

(*Slowly Kerzhentsev's knees buckle. He falls to the floor and begins to cry, then to howl, louder and louder.*)

THIRD ACTRESS (*Opening her eyes, terrified*): Good God! You're not . . . are you . . . ?

(*Kerzhentsev begins wildly barking. He grabs the table-cloth with his teeth and pulls it off the table. One of the Attendants takes the sound-effects bag and tramples on it, producing the sound of breaking glasses, china, etc. General confusion.*

KERZHENTSEV (*Suddenly calms down, breathes normally for a moment, and asks weakly*): Where am I?
THIRD ACTOR: Vous êtes chez nous, with the Kurganovs.
THIRD ACTRESS (*Kneels in front of him, with concern*): Maestro, you do know who Irina Pavlovna Kurganova is? C'est moi.
KERZHENTSEV: Of course. What happened here?
THIRD ACTOR: You don't feel well . . . obviously a little indisposed . . .
KERZHENTSEV (*Looking around*): Has there been a raid? Cossacks?

THIRD ACTRESS: Pay no attention to it. It's nothing, the servants will take care of everything.

THIRD ACTOR: And don't worry, we've sent for the doctor.

KERZHENTSEV: Is somebody ill? Oh, I'm terribly sorry. (*Getting up*): In that case, I won't disturb you any longer. (*Kisses her hand.*) Dearest Irina Pavlovna! Dear Pavel Petrovich! Good night! (*He walks unsteadily away. The guests stand in frozen silence. Turning to the Professor*): I'm not sure they deserved such a realistic performance.

(*The guests leave the platform, and the First Actor, Savelyov, and the First Actress, Tatyana, take their places. Kerzhentsev is helped into Hamlet's doublet. He takes a belt from which hangs an empty sword case.*)

Good morning, mon ami.

FIRST ACTOR: Good morning, Anton. What happened last night?

KERZHENTSEV: What do you mean, what happened?

FIRST ACTOR: Well, at the Kurganovs'!

KERZHENTSEV: I don't understand. Oh, somebody was ill, so I left. Anyhow, I don't care for them very much.

FIRST ACTOR (*Worriedly patting him on the back*): You really shouldn't drink so much. Certainly not before your opening night.

SECOND ACTOR: Alexey Konstantinovich, would you care to take a look at the wigs?

FIRST ACTOR: Oh yes, of course. (*To Kerzhentsev*): I'll be right back.

KERZHENTSEV (*To the Professor*): You see I could have lost my mind, he wouldn't have noticed anything. But she?

FIRST ACTRESS: Anton Ignatyevich—

KERZHENTSEV (*Turns quickly*): Yes?

FIRST ACTRESS: You weren't drunk last night?

KERZHENTSEV: Do you think I was?

FIRST ACTRESS: I've never seen you drunk.

KERZHENTSEV: Maybe I drink secretly.

FIRST ACTRESS: Oh, I don't believe that. That's not like you.

KERZHENTSEV: Oh, you know what I'm like? (*Intensely*): Do you think you know me, Tatyana Nikolayevna?

FIRST ACTRESS: I wanted to talk to you about something else.

KERZHENTSEV: What?

FIRST ACTRESS: For some time it's seemed to me as if you were—

KERZHENTSEV: Why don't you finish it?

FIRST ACTRESS (*Pause*): —ill.

KERZHENTSEV: And do you, by any chance, know the name of my illness?

FIRST ACTRESS: No, but I'm worried about you.

KERZHENTSEV: You're worried about me? Why?

FIRST ACTRESS: Why shouldn't I be? I'm a human being, Anton Ignatyevich. I don't like to suffer, and I don't like it when other people suffer.

KERZHENTSEV (*To the Professor*): She said it so simply, so simply, that at that moment an equally simple question occurred to me.

PROFESSOR: What question?

KERZHENTSEV: Not that I regretted what I started, I never regret anything, but suddenly I asked myself: is it all worth it? I suddenly had the feeling that there must be another way out. Tatyana Nikolayevna!

FIRST ACTRESS: Yes?

KERZHENTSEV (*Intensely*): Tatyana Nikolayevna, do you love your husband very much?

FIRST ACTRESS: You know that!

KERZHENTSEV: Yes, yes . . . Tell me only one thing, why don't you believe me?

FIRST ACTRESS: But Anton Ignatyevich, do you think one can believe you?

KERZHENTSEV (*Laughs*): Right. Let's forget it.

FIRST ACTRESS (*Laughs, relieved*): Yes. Let's forget it— both of us. D'accord?

(*First Actor returns; Kerzhentsev grabs his arm.*)

KERZHENTSEV: Mr. Prosecuting Attorney, I looked at Tatyana Nikolayevna, and I couldn't resist thinking: I could kill you too, and nothing would happen to me —and I felt something new, pleasant, and at the same time a little frightening. Man was no longer something untouchable for me. As if the protective covering had fallen off, he was now naked and bare, and to kill him seemed seductive, easy. Still, to kill *her*, what sense would that make? If she loved him so desperately, as she claimed, then his death would be a hundred times worse punishment for her . . . (*He lets the First Actor go, and answers the First Actress*): D'accord! You can count on it! Done!

FIRST ACTOR: What's done?

FIRST ACTRESS: I told Anton Ignatyevich that we're worried about him. And he promised me—no, actually he didn't promise me anything.

FIRST ACTOR: Well then! (*Turns to Kerzhentsev*): Why don't you promise us that you will go to a good doctor as soon as possible? Promise me, so that you don't have to say adieu to Hamlet.

KERZHENTSEV: Do you want to play him?

FIRST ACTOR: No, I want you to play him. But don't get carried away.

KERZHENTSEV: What do you mean?

FIRST ACTOR: Well, you might stab somebody.

KERZHENTSEV: What are you talking about?

FIRST ACTOR: That . . . you might *stab* somebody. You might take the sword and actually run somebody through.

KERZHENTSEV: With this sword? It's blunt . . .

FIRST ACTOR: You don't say . . . (*He draws the imaginary sword out of Kerzhentsev's sheath.*) Here, try it! Make a thrust and you'll see! (*He presents Kerzhentsev with the imaginary sword.*)

FIRST ACTRESS: Alexey! Please! Please, stop it!

FIRST ACTOR: What? What's the matter, Tanya?

FIRST ACTRESS: You know quite well I don't like jokes like this.

FIRST ACTOR (*Laughs*): I'm sorry. Forgive me, both of you.

KERZHENTSEV: It was your idea, Alexey. "Make a thrust." (*To the Professor*): He sealed his own fate. (*He accompanies them off the platform.*) Now, there's only one thing left to do: to gain an official absolution of all my past and future sins—a medical certificate of my illness. You'll be surprised to find, Mr. Prosecuting Attorney, that this certificate is going to be made out by no less than the head of the Psychiatric Clinic of the St. Elizabeth Institute for Nervous Disorders, Professor Drzhembitsky, in person. (*To the Actors*): Who wants to play him, gentlemen?

(*Everybody looks to the Professor, who, without hesitation, rises and goes to the platform.*)

PROFESSOR: If you don't mind, I will take this part myself.

KERZHENTSEV: Not at all, it's a pleasure, Professor. If you don't mind playing a fool.

PROFESSOR: That can't be helped. (*He takes his place behind a white table.*) We have discussed all the possible genetic influences, Mr. Kerzhentsev; we have also discussed your own character image. Now, before I dare to make my deduction, allow me to return to the embarrassing matter of the soirée at Kurganov's?

KERZHENTSEV: But of course! Unfortunately, I can give you only very incomplete information about it.

PROFESSOR: One thing interests me above all: the participants are agreed that at the onset of your fit you howled.

KERZHENTSEV: So?

PROFESSOR: Yes, howled! Then you barked! Surely, then, we can also agree that such behavior in a normal human being is very unusual.

KERZHENTSEV: Sorry I can't share your opinion, Professor. Why shouldn't a normal human being howl if he feels like it?

PROFESSOR: That's quite an extraordinary thought, Mr. Kerzhentsev. But you really should speak more specifically of the causes, because howling, as we know, is an expression of dogs—or wolves. You will—being an actor —agree with me that human beings have more subtle means of expression at their command.

KERZHENTSEV: I'm not going to argue with you, Professor. But it seems to me, every expression equals the experience. It's hypocrisy that forces a bourgeois to reduce himself to a definite socially sanctioned scale of behavior. Why should a human being without conventional scruples—that is, a normal human being—if he suffers like a dog, not howl like a dog?

PROFESSOR (*Quickly*): May I ask then, what do you actually suffer from?

KERZHENTSEV: I? From nothing you could define concretely. I spoke in general. *Only* in general, Professor.

PROFESSOR: But where are the boundaries of human behavior? Ultimately, you might get it into your head to crawl around on all fours.

KERZHENTSEV: What's wrong with that?

PROFESSOR: It would definitely not be usual.

KERZHENTSEV: Not be usual! There it is again—that famous formula, that incantation of the bourgeoisie! I'm being open with you, Professor, and I deserve the same openness. Be honest with me: did you never, not once in your life, crave to crawl around on all fours?

PROFESSOR: I'm afraid I have to disappoint you.

KERZHENTSEV: Never mind! In your profession you're forced to witness so many tragedies, it's quite possible you might still have the opportunity.

PROFESSOR: But why? What could possibly make me do that? Won't you take me into your confidence, Mr. Kerzhentsev?

KERZHENTSEV (*Motions him closer, whispers conspiratorially*): You may feel something quite unexpectedly, at a party, or at home at tea time, something you have never ever felt before; namely, that you have legs, and that in those legs something extraordinary is happening, that your knees are buckling under a strange, unexplainable weight, and then . . . tell me frankly, Professor Drzhembitsky . . . it'll be our secret. When you suddenly simply want to crawl around on the floor a little bit, do you think that anything could hold you back?

PROFESSOR: Mr. Kerzhentsev, don't you think you should rest a little?

KERZHENTSEV: If a woman said that to me I'd know what she was offering. What's your offer, one of your warm, friendly cells, in isolation?

PROFESSOR: God forbid! God forbid! No. I didn't have that in mind at all.

KERZHENTSEV (*Turning to the First Actor*): That was exactly what he had in mind! And he would have done it without hesitation if I hadn't been *the* Anton Ignat-yevich Kerzhentsev. What I said to him in a harmless conversational tone sounded so absurd, even to him, that he had to ask himself: "What if this is all just a crazy actor's prank?" What would your learned colleagues, your students, your enemies say then? True, Professor Drzhembitsky?

PROFESSOR: As long as you digress, you will allow me to do the same. A psychiatrist, Mr. Kerzhentsev, must proceed more carefully than other doctors. Under certain circumstances a hasty accommodation in our Institute could change a condition from the latent to the acute.

KERZHENTSEV (*Excitedly to the First Actor*): Ah, there we come right to the point, Mr. Prosecuting Attorney. Before anyone will risk making a hasty diagnosis that someone is mad, it's much more convenient to let him go ahead and kill. But why then, afterwards, do we try to make madmen out of murderers?

PROFESSOR: You're mistaken. That definitely was not my intention. Out of many symptoms, I—that is, Professor Drzhembitsky—concluded: If in your case it is indeed a matter of a psychic disturbance, it will rather manifest itself introvertively; that means, it will play itself out almost entirely within you, without penetrating to the outside world.

KERZHENTSEV: Too bad—in all that, he made only one tiny mistake. He saw me as a plain lunatic. What he didn't see was that I only *played* a lunatic, to be free to take revenge and strike at the outer world. Shall we go back to your office . . . (*Prompting*): "God forbid."

PROFESSOR (*Continuing from his script*): Oh, God forbid! That wasn't what I had in mind at all! What I would like to propose to you is an extensive period of rest, at home, with fine care. Do you have a house-keeper?

KERZHENTSEV: No, I prefer solitude; it is my unassailable castle. I'm at my best there—behind those high walls, in the company of my own thoughts.

PROFESSOR: I understand . . . but at least for a little while you should get yourself a housekeeper, and if you'll take my advice, she should definitely be young and pretty. If I were you, Mr. Kerzhentsev, I wouldn't underestimate that side of life. Say what you will, women bring a crucial harmony into our lives. They somehow contrive to make our knees buckle under quite a different weight than the one you just described so vividly. (*Offers his hand.*) Goodbye, Mr. Kerzhentsev.

KERZHENTSEV: Thanks! A thousand thanks, Professor. (*Turns to the First Actor*): He gave me a splendid idea. I decided to employ Tatyana Nikolayevna as housekeeper.

FIRST ACTRESS: Tatyana? That couldn't be right, Professor. I don't have that in my script.

PROFESSOR: It is there, madame. I assume it's connected with the role of Marya Vassilyevna.

SECOND ACTRESS: That's my role.

PROFESSOR: Well then, would you be so kind— (*Motions her to the platform.*)

SECOND ACTRESS: But . . . I don't understand any of it.

PROFESSOR: Don't be afraid. Just give yourself to the situation.

KERZHENTSEV (*Leaps on to the bed*): What was your name again?

SECOND ACTRESS: Marya Vassilyevna, your honor.

KERZHENTSEV: Let me look at you! Your hands! Turn around! Your teeth. Good! Good! . . . Now, Marya Vassilyevna—they told you I was ill. Right?

SECOND ACTRESS: Yes, your honor.

KERZHENTSEV: But I'm not ill. Do you understand?

SECOND ACTRESS: Yes, your honor.

KERZHENTSEV: I am an actor—how many nights did I say: What a piece of work is a man, how noble in reason, how infinite in faculty, in action how like an angel! in apprehension how like a god!—and that makes me very sad. Do you understand?

SECOND ACTRESS: Yes, your honor, I'll try.

KERZHENTSEV: You don't understand anything. But why should you? You'll be well taken care of by me if you don't wonder about anything. Do you think you can do that?

SECOND ACTRESS: Well, I can only try to do my best— your hon—

KERZHENTSEV: All right then, let's try. From now on I am going to call you Tatyana Nikolayevna. Do you understand? All right, what's your name?

SECOND ACTRESS: Tatyana Nikanorovna . . .

KERZHENTSEV: Nikolayevna, you dumb goose! But you don't need to remember the name. You're not going to introduce yourself to anybody. What you do have to remember is to call me Anton. But *only* when my eyes are closed. And you have to make love to me. Above all, you have to *love* me.

SECOND ACTRESS: Yes, your honor.

KERZHENTSEV: Well then! I'm lying on the bed and you enter the room. (*He closes his eyes.*) Anybody here?

SECOND ACTRESS: Yes.

KERZHENTSEV: Who is it? (*Sits up.*) Is it you, Tatyana Nikolayevna?

SECOND ACTRESS: Yes, your honor.

KERZHENTSEV (*Opens his eyes and screams*): Wrong! One more mistake and I'm going to throw you out!

SECOND ACTRESS: Oh, forgive me, your honor—

KERZHENTSEV: Anton!

SECOND ACTRESS (*Frightened*): Your eyes are open, your honor!

KERZHENTSEV: What? Oh! Oh! (*He closes his eyes.*) Is it you, Tatyana Nikolayevna?

SECOND ACTRESS: Yes—Anton.

KERZHENTSEV: Oh, dearest Tatyana . . . A violin! I need a violin!

(*The Violinist begins to play a sonata. Kerzhentsev reaches out blindly for the Second Actress. She reaches for him. He kisses her hands feverishly.*)

I knew you'd come! I knew it! I was expecting you. No, don't say anything. Sit down next to me and don't let go of my hand! (*She sits.*) At last you believe me! Thank you! Yes, I understand, I always seemed so proud to you, so unapproachable, you couldn't imagine that I could really love anyone. And yet the explanation was so simple, so simple. As the earth is in need of two poles to turn on its axis, so I needed you, the very embodiment of feeling, to balance the relentless force of my mind. (*He laughs.*) Men go into ecstasy at the sight of a snowy mountain peak; if only they knew more about themselves, all the miracles of the world would not astonish them so much as their own power to think. No, my dearest Tatyana, I'm not really ill. I confess to you, I lay down on my bed only to be alone with an idea—a thought—which would not let go of me. An idea as pure and noble as you are, Tatyana, giving itself to me like a passionate mistress. And yet, how strange, you've come and the idea retreats, fades—and can you imagine—I don't even care! Because with you, the memory of a scene came back. Something I must have seen once: a little girl and a little dog . . . frightened of each other in such a touching way—(*Intensely*): Tanya, will you stay with me forever?

SECOND ACTRESS (*Partly to Professor, partly to Kerzhentsev*): I don't know . . . I don't know.

KERZHENTSEV (*Tears away from her and falls on the bed without opening his eyes*): Then you should know what kind of a thought you're giving me up to. I'm going to kill your husband, Tatyana Nikolayevna, don't try to change my mind, it's all decided. Believe me, I don't like doing it. I don't even hate him; since my decision was made I've had a very unusual, close relationship with him, like father and son. I'm happy that he lives, drinks, eats. I'm happy that he's happy the way I want him to be for as long as I still allow him to live. I'm even concerned about his health. It's unforgivable to let him go out in this damp weather without galoshes, and I implore you, take better care of him. I say that, in spite of the fact that it will make my task more difficult. I remember, when I was a medical student, I was given a healthy dog, with straight, perfect legs, and I had a terrible battle with my conscience before I could skin him as the experiment required—alive. To this day I can still hear his howls . . . (*The Professor makes a note. The Second Actress begins to cry.*) Good God, you're crying? Why?

SECOND ACTRESS (*To the Professor*): I'm afraid.

KERZHENTSEV (*Sitting up*): You're afraid? And I've longed so to protect you from fear and suffering! Why do you force me to do the opposite? Why?

SECOND ACTRESS: I don't know . . . I don't know anything.

KERZHENTSEV: It would take so little, Tatyana Nikolayevna, so little. Give me your lips, your arms, give yourself to me—let me have your feelings—and my mind will be defenseless and at peace again; we'll be frightened of each other like the little girl and the little dog. . . . Will you?

SECOND ACTRESS: Yes . . . Yes . . .

KERZHENTSEV: You really want to?

SECOND ACTRESS: I will give you everything . . . but not my feelings . . .

KERZHENTSEV: Oh, my love! (*He throws her on the bed, but rises immediately, silences the violin, and turns to the others*): It may seem strange to you, my friends, but those were the happiest days of my life. What probably seemed even to the simple Marya Vassilyevna a sign of pure madness was really nothing but a new proof that my brain was working as reliably as a Swiss watch. The power of my imagination cast Tatyana Nikolayevna down onto my bed again and again, day after day, night after night, without my ever—and I repeat this because I can feel your astonishment—without my ever once being distracted from my intent. I couldn't be distracted by substitutes. No, I held her in my arms and made her cry out with lust, but at the same time—at the same time—I was free, soaring with my idea high above the earth . . . and then, even before the time was up— the time I allowed to pass to avoid suspicion, as if ordered by me—Savelyov appeared, to direct his own fate.

FIRST ACTOR (*Enters wearing a long coat and galoshes, carrying an umbrella*): I just wanted to ask how you were, Kerzhentsev, but I see you're better than ever.

(*The Second Actress gets up from the bed and modestly arranges her clothes.*)

KERZHENTSEV: I can't remember ever being sick. But since everyone else seems to know better, I adjusted myself to that as well as I could.

FIRST ACTOR: You really adjusted yourself to it quite well. I take my hat off to you. Why don't you introduce me to your charming friend?

KERZHENTSEV: She is my housekeeper.

FIRST ACTOR (*Dryly*): How practical. And what's your name, little one?

(*Kerzhentsev closes his eyes and waits.*)

SECOND ACTRESS: Tatyana Nikolayevna.

FIRST ACTOR: What?

KERZHENTSEV (*Opening his eyes*): That's the first time I've heard *that*. What's your name?

SECOND ACTRESS (*Confused*) : Marya Vassilyevna, your honor.

KERZHENTSEV: Go. You can go. Make us tea.

SECOND ACTRESS: Whatever you say, your honor. (*Leaves.*)

FIRST ACTOR: What was that?

KERZHENTSEV: She's mad. She just—dreams up new names. I hired her to have a *real* lunatic to observe. There's nothing wrong with that, I get along better with her than with normal people.

FIRST ACTOR: Anton, I never said that you were—

KERZHENTSEV: You said that I was capable of taking a sword and running it through somebody!

FIRST ACTOR: That was a silly joke. I never thought you'd take it so seriously.

KERZHENTSEV: But you *did* send me to the doctor.

FIRST ACTOR: Not I, Kerzhentsev, you're mistaken.

KERZHENTSEV: Then—Tatyana Nikolayevna! Isn't that the same?

FIRST ACTOR: She was worried about your health. What's wrong with that? She likes you.

KERZHENTSEV: Oh, yes? Well, I'm glad.

FIRST ACTOR: And it was she who sent me to you now.

KERZHENTSEV: She? Why?

FIRST ACTOR: The Queen is waiting for her son.

KERZHENTSEV: Her son?

FIRST ACTOR: Hamlet.

KERZHENTSEV: Hamlet? You haven't opened yet?

FIRST ACTOR: We're waiting for you. Can you imagine a more ideal return to life and the stage? Hamlet! Seemingly insane and yet far saner than everyone around him. We both felt we owed you that. Don't say no, Kerzhentsev. I beg you as a friend.

KERZHENTSEV: I won't deny it. You did hurt my feelings. What you both thought was madness was only a rebellion against intolerable conventions. And for that you nearly had me locked up in a madhouse.

FIRST ACTOR: Anton . . .

KERZHENTSEV: Let it go. I don't mean to blame anyone. I, too, love you. You know what I often thought as I sat here by my window watching the autumnal rain come down? I just hope Savelyov has his galoshes on.

FIRST ACTOR: As you see . . .

KERZHENTSEV: Good. I was afraid you might catch cold.

FIRST ACTOR (*Moved*): Kerzhentsev, forget all that's happened?

KERZHENTSEV: I will, gladly.

FIRST ACTOR: Bon. I'll set the rehearsal for tomorrow.

KERZHENTSEV: And wilt thou dull thy sword, Polonius?

FIRST ACTOR: On the contrary, my Prince, I'll see that it's sharpened. (*He embraces Kerzhentsev.*)

KERZHENTSEV (*Looking past him*): Adieu, Alexey Konstantinovich! God knows, even now I feel no more for you than regret. Yes, I regret that you aren't at least a better artist. If you were, I swear, I wouldn't kill you in spite of everything. There is so much darkness that we need every mind which helps to light the way. But you have no talent.

FIRST ACTOR: Rest you well—for your first rehearsal.

KERZHENTSEV: Rest you even better—for your last one.

FIRST ACTOR (*Laughs and bows*): "My honourable lord, I will most humbly take my leave of you."

KERZHENTSEV (*Bows also*): "You cannot, sir, take from me any thing that I will more willingly part withal: except my life, except my life, except my life."

(*There is the usual hubbub before rehearsal starts. All take their places. Musicians tune their instruments. The Attendants try the lights and put up partial set pieces. The Actors change their costumes, makeup, put on wigs, etc.*)

KERZHENTSEV (*Breathes in the familiar air deeply, stretches his arms, and shouts joyously*): At last!

(*The Attendants rush toward him and help him into Hamlet's costume.*)

PROFESSOR: And how did you sleep, Mr. Kerzhentsev?

KERZHENTSEV: Thank you for asking, Professor. Like a child, and, of course, alone. I didn't need my dream substitute anymore since reality was waiting for me with the dawn. At last!

FIRST ACTRESS (*In costume of the Queen*): Good morning, Anton Ignatyevich. At last, I'm glad to see you again.

KERZHENTSEV (*Kissing her hand*): Did you miss me, by any chance, Tatyana Nikolayevna?

FIRST ACTRESS: On stage, very much so.

KERZHENTSEV: But otherwise, very little?

FIRST ACTRESS: You know the friends of my husband are my friends as well.

KERZHENTSEV: Yes, that's why I'm happy to count myself among the friends of his friends.

FIRST ACTOR (*In the costume of Polonius*): Welcome, Kerzhentsev. (*He embraces him.*) At last, everybody I

like is here together again. You're welcome, all! Shall
we start?

KERZHENTSEV: I'm ready.

FIRST ACTOR: Splendid. Let's start. We'll see each other
again after the fifth act. (*He claps his hands.*)

(*The Musicians play a prelude. The Fourth Actress
enters, obviously as the Prologue in "Savelyov's production."*)

FOURTH ACTRESS (*Gong*): Act One, Scene One, Elsinore.
A Terrace in the Castle.

(*The Second and Fourth Actors now enter onto the
platform from opposite sides.*)

SECOND ACTOR: "Who's there?"

FOURTH ACTOR: "Nay, answer me: stand, and unfold
yourself."

SECOND ACTOR: "Long live the king!"

FOURTH ACTOR: "Bernardo?"

SECOND ACTOR: "You, Francisco?"

FOURTH ACTOR:
"You come most carefully upon your hour.
For this relief much thanks: 'tis bitter cold,
And I am sick at heart."

KERZHENTSEV: This is the way the end of my story begins, honored friends, and I am the only one who knows
that this time Hamlet is not just a play, but an infernal
machine which will explode precisely in the fourth
scene of the third act.

(*The Musicians play an intermezzo. As the Second and
Fourth Actors leave the platform, the First Actress and
the First and Third Actors take their places.*)

FOURTH ACTRESS (*Gong*): Act Two, Scene Two. A
Room in the Castle.

THIRD ACTOR: "We will try it."

FIRST ACTRESS: "But look where sadly the poor wretch comes reading."

FIRST ACTOR: "Away, I do beseech you both, away: I'll board him presently."

(*The First Actress and the Third Actor leave the platform as Hamlet [Kerzhentsev] now enters, book in hand.*)

How does my good Lord Hamlet?"

KERZHENTSEV: "Well, God-a-mercy."

FIRST ACTOR: "What do you read, my lord?"

KERZHENTSEV: "Words, words, words."

FIRST ACTOR: "Do you know me, my lord?"

KERZHENTSEV: "Excellent well; you are a panderer."

FIRST ACTOR: "Not I, my lord."

KERZHENTSEV: "Then I would you were so honest a man."

FIRST ACTOR: "Honest, my lord!"

KERZHENTSEV (*Stops the play and turns to the Professor*): Honest! Why didn't he stay a law student? He could have become a defense lawyer, or a judge, but he'll never be a good scapegoat. If he *had* to become an actor, why did he bring me onto the stage? But since he did, why is *he* still on it? Why is he directing this play that seals his fate? (*He returns to the platform.*) "It is true, Polonius, you played once i' the university?"

FIRST ACTOR: "That did I, my lord, and was accounted a good actor."

KERZHENTSEV: "What did you enact?"

FIRST ACTOR: "I did enact Julius Caesar: I was killed i' the Capitol; Brutus killed me." (*He exits.*)

KERZHENTSEV: I continued to speak clearly, precisely . . . separating my thoughts from the rhymes, but at that instant I stopped being an actor. . . . In the second scene of the third act, I suddenly knew: only twelve pages of paper separate me from the moment when I will become a murderer.

(*Gong*)

KERZHENTSEV (*As Hamlet*):
"Tis now the very witching time of night,
When churchyards yawn, and hell itself breathes out
Contagion to this world: now could I drink hot blood,
And do such bitter business as the day
Would quake to look on. Soft! now to my mother,
O heart, lose not thy nature; let not ever
The soul of Nero enter this firm bosom:
Let me be cruel, not unnatural."

(*Gong. He leaves the scene.*)

FOURTH ACTRESS: Act Three, Scene Three. Another Room in the Castle.
KERZHENTSEV: No longer an abstraction, Professor, no, my whole body relives the life process taking place in Alexey—the beating of his heart, the pulsing of the blood in his temples, the soundless rhythms of his brain. As soon as this process is interrupted, the heart stops beating, pumping blood, and the brain stops—but at what thought?

(*First and Third Actors enter.*)

FIRST ACTOR:
"My lord, he's going to his mother's closet;
Behind the arras I'll convey myself,
To hear the process; I'll warrant she'll tax him home:
And, as you said, and wisely was it said,
'Tis meet that some more audience than a mother,

Since nature makes them partial, should o'erhear
The speech, of vantage. Fare you well, my liege:
I'll call upon you ere you go to bed,
And tell you what I know."

THIRD ACTOR: "Thanks, dear my lord." (*He kneels to pray.*)

KERZHENTSEV: Never before had I reached such depth and intensity of insight. Not ever before had I had this all-encompassing feeling of a precisely poised, yet mercurial, self. And then and there—please don't take this for blasphemy—I understood what it means to be God. Without seeing I saw, without hearing I heard, and without thinking I understood.

THIRD ACTOR (*Rising from prayers*):
"My words fly up, my thoughts remain below:
Words without thoughts never to heaven go."

(*Exits.*)

FOURTH ACTRESS (*Gong*): Act Three, Scene Four. The Queen's Chamber.

(*The Musicians play a dramatic interlude.*)

KERZHENTSEV (*Rising*): God be with you, Alexey.

FIRST ACTOR: Give me a moment.

KERZHENTSEV (*Startled*): He stopped the rehearsal. Good God! Is this a sign from you? You don't want to let me have him?

FIRST ACTOR: Excuse me, friends, I'll be right back. (*He exits.*)

KERZHENTSEV: No . . . You've only granted him a five-minute postponement, and instead of praying, he's going—(*Laughs*)—to the toilet.

FIRST ACTRESS (*Steps toward Kerzhentsev and looks in the same direction he's looking*): How wonderfully the snow glistens. (*Looks directly at him.*) Anton Ignatyevich. (*His silence and his peculiar smile frighten her.*) Anton Ignatyevich.

FIRST ACTOR (*Returning*): We can continue.

FIRST ACTRESS: Alexey, Alexey! He's—

FIRST ACTOR: What's the matter with him? Anton!

KERZHENTSEV (*Getting control of himself*): Are you waiting for me? I don't begin this scene!

FIRST ACTRESS: No. I beg of you, no—

KERZHENTSEV (*Smiling*): Tatyana Nikolayevna obviously still thinks I really do intend to run you through.

FIRST ACTOR: Friends, friends, don't drag up what's already buried! There's no reason for it, and there's no time for it. Come on, let's continue! Queen and Polonius, Hamlet holding himself ready.

(*Gong. Musicians play the dramatic interlude again.*)

KERZHENTSEV: In the few seconds separating me from my entrance I understood—as only God could—the last things that would come: His brain would stop at the thought of *Her*. When he, as Polonius, frightened for the Queen, cries out, he will through the tapestry catch one last glimpse of Tatyana Nikolayevna. His brain would stop at the thought of *Her*. I knew then he would die, overwhelmed by love, and everything within me subsided, as in the last act of the tragedy. I was ready.

(*He disappears behind the scenery.*)

FIRST ACTOR:
"He will come straight. Look you lay home to him:
Tell him his pranks have been too broad to bear with,
And that your grace hath screen'd and stood between
Much heat and him. I'll sconce me even here.
Pray you, be round with him."

KERZHENTSEV (*Behind the scene*): "Mother, mother, mother!"

FIRST ACTRESS: "I'll warrant you; fear me not. Withdraw, I hear him coming."

(*First Actor hides behind the sheeting representing the tapestry.*)

KERZHENTSEV:
"Now, mother, what's the matter?"
FIRST ACTRESS:
"Hamlet, thou hast thy father much offended."
KERZHENTSEV:
"Mother, you have my father much offended."
FIRST ACTRESS:
"Come, come, you answer with an idle tongue."
KERZHENTSEV:
"Go, go, you question with a wicked tongue."
FIRST ACTRESS:
"Why, how now, Hamlet!"
KERZHENTSEV:
"What's the matter now?"
FIRST ACTRESS:
"Have you forgot me?"
KERZHENTSEV:
"No, by the rood, not so:
You are the queen, your husband's brother's wife;
And—would it were not so!—you are my mother."
FIRST ACTRESS:
"Nay, then, I'll set those to you that can speak."
KERZHENTSEV:
"Come, come, and sit you down; you shall not budge;
You go not till I set you up a glass
Where you may see the inmost part of you."

(*He reaches for the place where the sword should be.*)

FIRST ACTRESS:
"What wilt thou do? thou wilt not murder me?
Help, help, ho!"
FIRST ACTOR (*From behind the sheeting*):
"What, ho! help, help, help!"
KERZHENTSEV (*Drawing an imaginary sword*):
"How now! a rat? Dead, for a ducat, dead! Dead!"

(*He makes a graceful run at the arras and thrusts the imaginary sword with all his strength up to the hilt into it.*)

FIRST ACTOR:
"O, I am slain!"

(*First Actor falls immediately, but Kerzhentsev stabs him again and again. There are alarmed cries. The others rush toward Kerzhentsev and subdue him.*)

KERZHENTSEV (*Quietly*): Thank you, release me.

(*They look to the Professor. He nods; they release him. Kerzhentsev takes off his doublet.*) And that's all. C'est tout. Then I was arrested and brought into this house. And . . . decided to give you a full confession. (*He bows slightly. Takes his place.*)

PROFESSOR (*After a pause*): We have responded to your request, Mr. Kerzhentsev, and we have done all you wanted to give you every possibility of clarifying the circumstances of your actions. Nevertheless, there is still something which is beyond comprehension. Why did you so long and so carefully construct a plan which would guarantee you freedom from punishment, if today you confess everything so openly? You do know what you have to expect?
KERZHENTSEV: Yes, yes, I understand your surprise, but —something happened to me I didn't count on.

PROFESSOR: What was that?

KERZHENTSEV (*More to himself than to the others*): Imagine you live in a house with many rooms. You occupy only one of them, but you rightly assume that your will governs the entire house. Suddenly, you discover that somewhere, over there, in the other rooms, someone else is living. Some mysterious beings, maybe human, maybe something else, and the house actually *belongs* to these others. You want to protest, you want to rebel, you want, at least, to demand, to beg. But the door is closed, and behind it there is not a sound. And yet you know that there, behind that silent door, your fate is being decided.

PROFESSOR: Please clarify this further, Mr. Kerzhentsev.

KERZHENTSEV: I always considered my mind an impregnable fortress. But what if my impenetrable isolation is destroying me? Once I know that nothing and nobody is stronger than I, what happens when "I" become my own enemy? Who can help me then? Who will save me?

PROFESSOR: Do you know why you should become your own enemy?

KERZHENTSEV (*Suddenly very excited*): No . . . don't force me to answer that! Isn't it enough for you that I confessed? Mr. Prosecuting Attorney, if there is one ounce of humanity left in you, you won't deny me this: Turn me over to the courts! Prove to them that I am a sane man. Sane but a criminal! I have given you all the evidence you need. Aren't jealously and thirst for revenge motives for countless crimes? Haven't I proved that I loved Tatyana Nikolayevna passionately? Is it so implausible that her laughter offended me and that this offense, given my nature, would have unforeseeable consequences? Why don't you admit that I am an artist capable of identifying myself so totally with my character that I could lose control over myself? Is it so illogical that among so many amateurs behaving like Othello in daily life, there is one who lives his role to the end and kills? Let me go to prison! I don't repent killing Savelyov; I don't expect absolution from sin: I am irresistibly drawn by the mystical idea that in prison in the midst of men who have broken the law I will discover new, unknown springs of life—and become my own friend again. You will tell me—you must tell me that I'm sane!

PROFESSOR: There is one particular circumstance, Mr. Kerzhentsev, that you should know about. As far as I have been able to judge, you have, in your truth drama, reconstructed the entire story faithfully, *almost* to the letter. Only in one single scene did you depart considerably from reality.

KERZHENTSEV: No, Mr. Prosecuting Attorney, I swear I wrote the truth, nothing but the truth.

PROFESSOR: I'm sorry, but I have to insist. It is, unfortunately, a matter of the scene which had the gravest consequences.

KERZHENTSEV: Which one? Where's your proof? Do you have witnesses?

PROFESSOR: We have witnesses, Mr. Kerzhentsev, and that's why I must ask you to become an audience for a while. We will play the scene again for you in a changed version and you will have an opportunity to verify or contest it.

KERZHENTSEV: No, no!

PROFESSOR: Don't say no, Mr. Kerzhentsev, this may be the very scene that you yourself would like to see.

KERZHENTSEV: No . . .

PROFESSOR: Sit down, Mr. Kerzhentsev!

(*The Attendants place Kerzhentsev in a chair and put their hands on his shoulders.*)

PROFESSOR: You will understand that a change of cast is necessary. If you please, ladies and gentlemen!

(*The Musicians play the dramatic interlude again. Now the Fourth Actor takes the part of the First Actor, putting on the wig and costume of Polonius.*)

FOURTH ACTOR:
"He will come straight. Look you lay home to him:
Tell him his pranks have been too broad to bear with,
And that your grace hath screen'd and stood between
Much heat and him. I'll sconce me even here.
Pray you, be round with him."

FIRST ACTOR (*Playing Hamlet from behind the scene*):
"Mother, mother, mother!"

FIRST ACTRESS:
"I'll warrant you; fear me not. Withdraw, I hear him coming."

FIRST ACTOR (*Enters*):
"Now, mother, what's the matter?"

FIRST ACTRESS:
"Hamlet, thou hast thy father much offended."

FIRST ACTOR:
"Mother, you have my father much offended."

FIRST ACTRESS:
"Come, come, you answer with an idle tongue."

FIRST ACTOR:
"Go, go, you question with a wicked tongue."

FIRST ACTRESS:
"Why, how now, Hamlet!"

FIRST ACTOR:
"What's the matter now?"

FIRST ACTRESS:
"Have you forgot me?"

FIRST ACTOR:
"No, by the rood, not so:

You are the queen, your husband's brother's wife;
And—would it were not so!—you are my mother."
FIRST ACTRESS:
"Nay, then, I'll set those to you that can speak."
FIRST ACTOR (*A strange look in his eyes*):
"Come, come, and sit you down; you shall not budge;
You go not till I set you up a glass
Where you may see the inmost part of you."

(*He reaches for his sword.*)

FIRST ACTRESS:
"What wilt thou do? Thou wilt not murder me?
Help, help, ho!"
FOURTH ACTOR (*Behind tapestry*):
"What, ho! help, help, help!"
FIRST ACTOR (*Drawing imaginary sword*):
"How now! a rat? Dead, for a ducat, dead . . . dead . . ."

(*He wants to move toward the tapestry but is pulled to
the ground as if by a terrible force. Slowly he goes to
his hands and knees and begins to howl.*)

KERZHENTSEV (*Leaps up from his chair*): That is a lie!
(*The Attendants fight to hold him back.*) I killed him!
Call her, call my Tanya! She was there!
FIRST ACTOR (*Unable to restrain himself any longer, he
rushes toward Kerzhentsev*): Kerzhentsev, wake up!
She's here! She and I! I'm standing in front of you!
Don't you recognize me? I am not the Prosecuting
Attorney! I am Savelyov, the real Savelyov! Alive and
unharmed. Come to your senses! You must come to
your senses! It is all a nightmare coming from your wild
imagination . . .
KERZHENTSEV (*Stares into space*): Then it must have
happened . . . it *did* happen . . . you deserted me.
FIRST ACTOR: What? Who? We're all with you!

KERZHENTSEV (*Looks directly at him now, weakly*): My brain deserted me, Mr. Prosecuting Attorney, my rapier! It's not blunted but now someone else grips the hilt. And with deadly indifference it challenges me with a terrible question, me, the master, the creator: Have you pretended to be insane, to be able to kill—or have you killed because you are insane? And it answers me: You believed you were pretending but you are really mad. You are just the stupid, decadent little actor Kerzhentsev, just another actor, Kerzhentsev, the mad actor . . . (*He starts laughing.*)

(*The Professor signals an Attendant to close the curtain in front of Kerzhentsev.*)

PROFESSOR: I'm afraid our experiment failed, Mr. Savelyov. If there was ever a hope that the reconstruction of his imagined crime would bring order to his shattered mind, this hope is probably gone. He's locked himself firmly inside his fortress, and unless there's a miracle there is no help for him. In any case, thank you all for your extraordinary cooperation.

SECOND ACTOR: You will excuse us, Alexey Konstantinovich. We have a performance . . .

THIRD ACTOR: I will play for you tonight if you want me to.

SAVELYOV: What? Oh yes, yes, of course . . .

FOURTH ACTRESS: If there's anything we can do, Tatyana, you know . . .

THIRD ACTRESS: Tatyana Nikolayevna, I am sorry for you.

(*The Actors return their scripts, music sheets, and props, and exit, accompanied by the two Attendants.*)

SAVELYOV: What will happen to him?

PROFESSOR: He stays here.

SAVELYOV: How long?

(*The Professor shrugs his shoulders.*)

TATYANA: Unless there is a miracle . . . ? Didn't you say, Professor, unless there is a miracle?

PROFESSOR: A new medicine might become available, various kinds of shocks may help, or—in rare cases— time itself. Since the initial cause was loneliness, I'd set all my hope on human contact. Communication could one day set him free.

TATYANA: Could we stay for a moment to have a few words alone with him?

PROFESSOR: Of course. He's calm now. They're taking care of him. I'll wait for you in my office.

(*He leaves.*)

SAVELYOV (*Puzzled*): What is it, Tatyana?

TATYANA: Alexey Konstantinovich, I didn't believe him. I did not understand—that he really loved me.

SAVELYOV: Nor did I . . . nor that he really wanted to kill me.

TATYANA: But he didn't. It didn't happen. But I humiliated him, and no matter what else contributed— it was that which shattered his mind, and I want to do what I can for him. I want to make up for it. I have to. I want to tell him—

SAVELYOV: Tatyana—let *me* talk to him.

TATYANA: But you *will* say I'll be with him—I'll be back.

SAVELYOV: Yes.

TATYANA: I'll ask the Professor to allow me to spend time with him—to take care of him. Maybe after awhile he'll even allow him to be released—in my care!

SAVELYOV: Tanya . . .

TATYANA: If you should feel in any way that this is—

SAVELYOV: For God's sake, Tanya, I want to help him too, but—

TATYANA: You are a good man, that's why I love you, Alexey. I didn't want to come here—you wanted it. You begged me to come for his sake. And I'm begging you now to let me—just try to—to give him—

SAVELYOV: But you don't love him!

TATYANA (*Hesitant*): No. But I don't know what would have happened if I had believed him that day. I only know that I believe him today. He needs what nobody ever gave him . . . and I want him to know that I . . .

SAVELYOV (*Pleading*): Tanya . . . ?

TATYANA: Yes! I have decided, Alexey. Do you understand?

SAVELYOV: Yes . . . I'll talk to him.

TATYANA (*Kisses him*): Thank you! I'll speak to the Professor and arrange what has to be done and I'll see you at home . . . and . . . (*She goes.*)

(*Savelyov remains motionless for a moment. Then he goes to the platform and draws open the curtain. We see Kerzhentsev seated between the two Attendants with a faraway look in his eyes.*)

SAVELYOV: Kerzhentsev . . . so you really did kill me!